P9-EDR-651

THE CHARISMA CAMPAIGNS

Other books by Jack Matthews

Bitter Knowledge

An Almanac for Twilight

Hanger Stout, Awake!

Beyond the Bridge

The Tale of Asa Bean

Jack Matthews

THE CHARISMA CAMPAIGNS

Harcourt Brace Jovanovich, Inc.
New York

First edition
ISBN 0-15-116800-8
Library of Congress Catalog Card Number: 71-174511
Printed in the United States of America
B C D E

To Fran and Ralph Gauvey,
with years of good memories

THE CHARISMA CAMPAIGNS

1

I called Buckholz and Cripps into my office at about two-thirty.

There weren't any customers on the lot, except for two college boys looking at a VW. Just window-shopping. It was a fine afternoon, sunny with a nice breeze blowing from the south, and it was only March. Cripps was standing beside me, smoking a Marlboro cigarette, and both of us were watching Bucky, who had just started back towards the office. He had been watching the college boys, after asking them if they wanted help. They said they didn't, and then I yelled out to Buckholz.

Now he was swinging himself towards us with his knees looking like they were fastened together, the way the legs of some fat men look. His tie was blowing over his shoulder. Buckholz never wears a tie clip. Cripps wears a bow tie all the time, and I wear a string tie. Occasionally someone makes a remark on the fact that the three of us all wear different kinds of ties.

When Bucky came up, I said, "Fist Hit by Chin, Man Injured."

Bucky said, "What's up, Rex?"

"Bucky," I said, "you just don't have any interest in current events. How about this one: 'Truck Driver Swerves to Avoid Child, Falls Off Sofa.' "

Bucky laughed a little, and said, "Well, I've heard that one, too."

"That's what I call the old one-two," I said.

Neither one of them answered that one, so I said, "Well, should we go in the office out of the wind, or talk out here?"

"I kind of like the sunlight," Cripps said, and Bucky nodded his chin up and down in his fat neck.

"It's like this," I said, punching my index finger in the palm of my other hand. "I want May to be the biggest month we've ever had."

"Sounds good to me," Cripps said. He spun his cigarette off against the side of a '66 Comet we had just taken in.

"And I've got a sales angle that will send all three of us on fabulous Florida vacations next winter if we can live up to it."

Buckholz pulled his pants legs up and leaned back against one of the white poles that we use to light up the lot at night. "Sounds good; what is it?" Bucky said. His voice is so high and husky, it sometimes reminds me of a woman with a bad cold.

"Those bass I stocked my lake with should be up to

about three pounds this summer," I said. "And I got all those Scotch pines and red pines the state helped me plant a couple years ago. They're big enough to cover the hill in back, and of course there's all kinds of trees around the lake itself."

Before I could explain any farther, a '67 Pontiac came up and a young man and woman got out. Cripps started to move off towards them, but I told him to wait a minute.

"Let 'em look around a little first," I said. "Anyway, I want you both to hear my plan. They're your customers, though, Cripps. Right, Bucky?"

Buckholz hitched his pants up a little higher, so that his hairless calves glistened like half-gallon milk bottles. "Sure," he said.

Then once again I punched my palm with my index finger for emphasis, and said, "Everybody who buys a car from Rex McCoy's Car Sales during the sunny month of May, by God, *gets a free season ticket to fish on that lake!*"

"How about that!" Cripps said. "No kidding?"

"No kidding."

"That's really something, Rex!" Buckholz said, standing up straight. He stuck a toothpick in his mouth and squinted at me in the sunlight.

"How do you like this?" I went on. "I've got a slogan all ready: 'You get a free vacation with every car!' "

"Christ, Rex, that's great!" Bucky said. "Yes, I really like it."

"Everybody else pays a hundred fifty bucks for a season ticket at Wingback Lake. But you buy a car from Rex McCoy or one of his boys, and you get a season ticket free. We'll have them licking our hands."

"Is that what you're calling it?" Buckholz asked. "Wingback Lake?"

"Right. I think it's got a nice sound to it."

"I like it," Cripps said.

"I like it, too," Buckholz said. "Leave it to the old Mac."

"How about the wife?" Cripps asked. "How's she going to feel about having your summer place all messed up with fishermen?"

"Hell, you know how sensitive she is, and how she's always felt about that place," I said. "I could never get her to move out there with me. Or even go out there to fish. She's still trying to recover from some goddam mosquito bites she got once when she was in the Girl Scouts. She's just not the outdoor type; so I figure, why fight it? Not only that, I'll get more money out of that lake now in one summer than I would with ten years of crop shares on the land around it."

Bucky kind of frowned, and when I asked him what was the matter, he said, "What was this business about the state planting trees? Wasn't there something about you had to let the lake be open to the public three or four years?"

"Bucky," I said, "you've hit on the best part of the whole thing. I looked at that agreement close, and they can't keep me from this deal. First of all, I got it both ways. I'm *giving* a season's fishing to certain people who, it so happens, buy a car from us in May. Also, it's public because I am in fact offering for free the same season ticket to anybody . . . however, those people who don't happen to buy a car from us in May will have to pay a toll charge to get to the lake, and they can only pay for it on a seasonal basis —or a hundred and fifty bucks. That's a private road they have to go on to reach the lake—you both remember it, don't you?—and old Metzger, the farmer next to me who owns half the road, will share in the profits. I got an agreement with him to accept fifty bucks for every paying customer—if we have any—and to allow all the others, the ones who buy cars in May, to get in free."

"Christ," Bucky said, turning away from us and laughing and shaking his head.

"I'll have everything down on paper, you can be sure of that," I told them.

"No doubt about *that!*" Bucky said, still laughing. "Man, you're number one!"

"The Only Thing Local Dealer Has Against Rich," I said, "Is Their Money."

Then Cripps walked off to wait on the couple who had driven up in the Pontiac, but they were just looking around. And along about four o'clock, which was a pretty slow time, I took Bucky over to Yerby's, where I bought him a double shot of Jack Daniel's, Green Label, with water, and had one myself.

I was feeling pretty good about everything, and when Bucky went back to the lot I told him to send Cripps over and I'd do the same for him.

So Cripps came in a few minutes later, and I had Yerby set up the J. D. and water again. Cripps is quiet and uncommunicative, and his eyes aren't quite straight. He isn't much of a salesman.

"You really like this new plan?" I asked him when we were halfway through the drinks.

"Yes, I think it'll work," Cripps said. "It's original at least. You've got to say that for it. It's got the stamp of McCoy genius."

When we finished our drinks, Cripps left, and I began to think about going home. I thought of my wife, and ordered another one. Maybe I would read my newspapers and eat right here at Yerby's, even though I didn't care much for the food. Still, one more double of J. D. would make anything edible. My leg was hurting, too, and another drink might help.

My wife thought the plan was screwy. That's exactly what she had said the night before: "Screwy."

"Wife Rejects Husband's Plan," I had said, and she said, "Oh, shut up!"

I'd be damned if I wanted to eat dinner with her.

2

About three weeks after that, Metzger came in. He was the farmer next to what was once supposed to have been our "country place." He was a serious-minded old duck, and he was wearing a broad-shouldered double-breasted suit that must have been thirty years old. I had seen him only in dirty work clothes until the day he came on the lot.

"Well, neighbor," I said. "Paying a visit?" Mr. Metzger said he was, and I told him to make himself at home. We stood there for a few minutes, talking about the weather—which I always do with farmers. But I noticed his eyes flicking out towards my line of cars while we were talking there. He seemed a little edgy, and I didn't want to flush him. I decided to calm him down with a little joke.

So when there was a pause in the conversation, I said, "Mr. Metzger, what are the last words you want to hear?"

He looked at me for a second as if I was really asking him a question, and I smiled to signal him that I was just telling a gag. Already I was sorry I had launched into this joke, because there were probably only about three chances in a thousand the old idiot would understand.

But I was too far in it now to back out. "What was that again?" he asked, moving half a step closer.

"I said, 'What are the last words you want to hear?' "

"The last words I want to hear," Mr. Metzger mused, grabbing his chin. "Guess I don't know, Mr. McCoy."

" 'Hello deh. Ah is yoh new NEIGH-buh.' "

I laughed loud enough for both of us, so that he would know the joke was over. And I turned away from him, so that I couldn't see whether he had gotten it or not, and rubbed a little dirt spot off the hood of a 1970 Cougar XR-7 we had just taken in. 351-cubic-inch V-8. Very clean.

When I turned back, old Metzger's face was perfectly composed and earnest; but I knew my joke had done the trick—it had broken the momentum of the old conversation and ended the ceremonies. Now we were getting down to business. Mr. Metzger told me he was interested in buying a car. It wouldn't have helped him any to wait for May to come around, even if he'd been a fisherman, because I had thrown in all fishing rights with the agreement we made about the road.

I showed him a '66 Buick, which appeared to have been run off a cliff when we got it in. It had 96,000 miles showing on it. All we did was put molasses oil in it, slap new rubber pads on the pedals, do a forty-dollar metallic-green paint job, and replace the three worst tires with white sidewall recaps. There was also about a hundred dollars of minimum body work done on it, but I got a special rate from Delanger's for that.

Metzger looked at the car almost all afternoon. He had said he wanted a late-model Buick, and all I had other than that one was two '68's. They were in a lot better condition, but for some reason Metzger liked that '66.

I didn't want to waste too much time on him, because I figured him for a hard buyer, so I told him to go ahead and look while I went back into the office to do some more work on the May sales campaign.

My wife didn't call it screwy any more. She just didn't pay any attention to it one way or the other. Once I told her, "You'd think you didn't have any idea where your bread and butter came from, the way you refuse to take any interest in my business."

But that didn't impress her. She told me she'd rather eat cake, and then she gave a dirty laugh. Her folks have always had money, and my sarcasm didn't work because it was literally true, what I said: she *didn't* know. She couldn't stand poor screwed-up Buckholz and Cripps, either. Any more than she liked the farm I bought . . . as an investment, it's true, but also with the idea that we could make it into a summer home. But all my wife could do on her first and only trip out there was lift her aristocratic nose, smell the mildew in the house, and that was it.

"Wife Scorns Husband's Gift," I said, and she gave a shudder that would have been a credit to Princess Grace at a farting match.

My wife and I fit each other like plaintiff and defendant. We were made for each other. She is a born victim, and I am a born victimizer, I guess. I have always been clumsy in little things. It seems like everywhere I go I'm stepping on somebody's feet and jabbing somebody with my elbow. I even punish my clothes; I rip shirts and pants, and break shoestrings and spill coffee, booze and cigar ashes all over everything I wear . . . not to mention innocent bystanders.

It's uncanny. I used to think there was some kind of hex over me, but soon I realized it was just my life style, that people talk about, and the way I was built. I am really, when you come right down to it, close to being an insensitive slob in my movements and gestures.

I'll never forget the way my wife and I first met. She was an accident looking for me to happen to her. It was in college. One time at the fraternity house we got into an impromptu, silly-ass tag game with the sorority house next door, and there was this pale and haughty-looking little sophomore, and when I was chasing her down the hill in front, my foot slipped in some leaves (it was October) and I went barreling into her, knocked her flat and sprained her ankle.

So that was how we met, my wife and I. After that first meeting, I would catch her every now and then gazing at me with long meditative stares. I could imagine her thinking: He Must Be the One, After All.

So we began dating, and on the dance floor I was always stepping on her feet, and the first time I kissed her I bruised her ribs. Once I was zipping her up in back, and I tore the zipper off, and another time I tripped over her feet in a lecture hall (it was botany, I think) and brought down about two rows of chairs.

But I was talking about that day at the lot when Mr. Metzger came in. I sat there in the office working on some past accounts, while old Metzger nosed around the '66 Buick. Our office is nothing more than a two-car garage I bought when Consolidated Building had a special sale on prefab garages seven years ago. I fixed it so they would put in an extra wall, with a door and three windows, for only three hundred additional. Inside the office were an electric stove, a rack of elk antlers on the wall, four wooden chairs, and a couple of good metal desks. Everything but the antlers had been bought at auctions, where I like to buy things.

Early in the afternoon, Bucky sold a '68 Dodge to a lady schoolteacher who walked with a cane, and Cripps sold a VW we had taken in for another VW. It was like trading two peas, because they were the same color. Cripps had all but closed this sale three days earlier, but was waiting for credit clearance on the buyer's father. The credit rating wasn't real good, but I let the sale go through anyway, because Cripps hasn't been doing too well. The buyer was a college boy named Williams, under age.

I was just thinking of a drink at Yerby's, when Metzger

came up to me and said, "I think I'll just buy that Buick of yours."

"Okay, Mr. Metzger," I answered, slapping my hands together two or three times, "I'll just sell that little honey to you."

I have always liked to sell a car. It's in my blood. I like to lay the papers out there neatly in front—the credit report (only, Metzger paid cash, like a lot of farmers), the license transfer, the title, the contract—and lay down a good Husky Grip Paper Mate ball-point pen beside them. Sometimes when I get ready to go into action, I take a couple seconds to look through the window of what was meant to be a double garage and size up the rolling stock we have lined up, all tuned, new-looking and shiny, in the lot. And, by God, I feel proud. Local Man Success at Car Trade. Last year, I made over forty-five thousand, which would have impressed a lot of people. My wife excluded.

I felt extra good sitting down there with old Metzger. For one thing, I figured I was getting rid of a real motorized hive of scratched junk. And from then on I wouldn't be seeing much of Metzger anyway. I knew I wasn't going to be doing much fishing at Wingback Lake. Not with all those people around.

3

One of the first signals came on May 4, when I went out to Wingback Lake to see how things were going. It was a fine sunny day, and I took my fishing equipment along, figuring I could get a couple hours' good fishing in on a day like this, before the place got jammed with satisfied used-car customers.

I had had a dock built, and a couple of used aluminum johnboats that I had bought at an auction put in the lake. This was so I could advertise boating as part of the season ticket.

I was down there on the dock, staring at about an inch and a half of dirty water in the bottom of one of the boats, when I heard a footstep on the dock. I turned around, and there was Metzger. I kind of froze up, because I was wondering how that '66 Buick I sold him was lasting.

But the old man seemed friendly. We exchanged some small talk, and then Metzger frowned and scratched his head. When he looked off in the distance, I knew he was about to bring up something that he figured was important.

"You know," he said, "that there Buick you sold me. That's some car!"

"Yes," I said tentatively. "You've got yourself some car there."

"I mean, it's the most comfortable car I ever owned. I told you Mother and I drove it to California last month, didn't I?" That's what he always called his wife, "Mother."

"Yes, I guess you did mention something," I said, trying to remember.

"Not a bit of trouble," Metzger said, his voice getting kind of faraway. "And only used three quarts of oil. Rode like a dream."

"Well, that's just fine. I knew it would make a sweetheart of a car for you."

"Like a dream," Metzger said, shaking his head wonderingly.

I was trying to think of what he had traded in for the Buick, but I couldn't remember that, either. It must have been a dog, though. Maybe it was one of the pack I sent to Cincinnati, where I periodically unload the dogs on one downtown dealer and buy good clean stock from three or four others. I pay a hundred, hundred twenty dollars more for the wholesale stock and sell fifty, sixty dollars cheaper. That's why I'm the best *independent* dealer, with the fastest low-profit turnover, in the whole state.

"Yes sir," Metzger went on, "I guess I owe you a great deal. Letting me have a bargain like that, and then just offering me fifty dollars flat for every customer that buys a season ticket to your lake here—just so's he can use our road. Giving me a free season ticket to fish and"—he stared at the water-filled rowboat a second—"boat on the lake. Of course I don't do much of that sort of thing, still . . . the thought's the thing. That's what Mother and I always believed."

"That's fine," I said, picking up my rod and tackle box. "Honesty Found Best Policy." I was feeling discouraged, what with the boats leaking and this windbag hanging around. Not only that, I was a little wary. I still figured there was about one chance in ten the old son of a bitch was being sarcastic. I had trouble believing that Buick had taken Mother and him to California on only three quarts of oil.

But when I glanced at him again, I saw that his face was peaceful and earnest. It didn't look like the face of a sarcastic man, and when I began to think about it, Mr. Metzger was the last man in the world to get sarcastic anyway.

"And I've decided something," he said. He was staring at the lake wisely. He nodded his head, and in the same movement shoved half a fistful of Mail Pouch chewing tobacco in his mouth.

"Yes sir, I've been thinking, Mr. McCoy, and I know how I can pay you back."

"How's that?"

"You got a pretty nice little setup here," Metzger went on, still nodding at the lake, like there were several old friends out there he recognized. "A puh-retty nice little setup."

"Not bad," I said, starting a little shuffle to get around him. But Mr. Metzger was standing there blocking the way, comfortably at ease, his hands folded inside his overalls bib, one side of his cheek bulged like a tumor with chewing tobacco.

"Except for one thing." When he said that, his little blue eyes snapped into place, and he seemed to be looking right inside my head, as far back as my ears, maybe. There was a little grin on his face, and at that instant I noticed how pink his skin was. It was like the skin of a healthy six-year-old, except for the peppering of beard on the lower half of his cheeks.

"Don't know what it is, do you?" he said.

"Well, can't say I do," I answered.

"A watchman."

"A watchman?"

Mr. Metzger closed his eyes and nodded his head. "That's right. Don't you know that *anybody* can come in here? What good does it do to have a season ticket, if anybody can come in anyway?"

While he stood there looking as wise as Winston Churchill or Bernard Baruch, I tried thinking of what I could say to him. Of course, I had thought of having somebody there, but the expense of hiring a man would have been ten times the loss incurred by casual lawbreakers. Not only that, I didn't *care* how many fishermen there were on the lake. As soon as the place became impossible, people would simply stop coming. It was a little bit like a governor on an engine.

It was obviously impossible to explain any of this to Mr. Metzger. It would either strike him as being too cynical, or he wouldn't understand at all. So I just stood there trying to think of a good, convincing lie, and while I was doing that, the old windbag said something that convinced me there would be no stopping him. Because he'd got this idea in his head that he owed me something.

"So *I'll* just keep an eye on it," he said.

"You'll what?"

"Me. You don't have no watchman, and I don't have no crops to put out next year, because the doctor says I shouldn't strain my heart, so I'll be your watchman myself."

"Why, I wouldn't think of asking you to do that," I told him.

"You haven't," he said. "I asked myself, and the answer was yes."

He thought this was kind of funny, so he repeated it, and then leaned over and let about a half-cup of well-masticated elixir of Mail Pouch chewing tobacco splat on the dock between us.

I tried to talk him out of it; but Mr. Metzger insisted, and finally I said he could go ahead and do it if he wanted to.

When I got in my car and started to drive away, I saw the old duck standing there on the bank with both of his hands still tucked in his overalls bib, staring contentedly out over the water as if he owned the place.

When he heard my car accelerate, he turned and waved. I waved back and then drove towards town, quickly forgetting about the old screwball.

Bygones Bygones, Used-Car Philosopher Claims.

4

A couple of days later, I went out on our flagstone patio, shaped like a big teardrop, to breakfast, and my wife was sitting there blowing on her coffee and staring thoughtfully in the air. She got up and put my bacon and four scrambled eggs in front of me, and then she cleared her throat and said, "Denise asked me to go to Spain with her."

I didn't say much, but made equivocal noises while I was eating, and after a while she went on. "She'll only be gone for five weeks. You know, I've told you about the tour they're taking. She's going to get to Madrid, and then they're going to tour the countryside. Even go to the Balearic Islands. It'll be a simply fantastic trip."

I still didn't say anything. When she turned away after refilling my coffee cup, I saw that her ears were red, so I realized I was getting to her. She had majored in Spanish in college, and the only place she had been to was Mexico, twice. She had let me know a number of times that the experience afforded by only two trips to Mexico wasn't much for a Spanish major.

"Well?" she said, after I lighted a Dutch Masters panetela. She hates for me to smoke cigars at breakfast. "Well," she said, "what do you think?"

"Think about what?" I asked her, pulling my cigar out of my mouth and looking surprised.

"Oh, you know perfectly well what I mean!"

"You mean about Spain?" I asked her.

"Yes," she said through her teeth, "about Spain."

"Well," I said, "I think it would make a pretty nice little trip for you, Mother."

There was an instant's silence, and then she said, "What did you call me?"

"I said it would make a pretty nice little trip, and I think you ought to go. You and Denise will have a great time. I can see you now: Madrid, Barcelona . . ."

"Yes, but what was it you just now called me?"

"I don't know. Let me see. I guess I called you 'Mother.' It must have slipped out."

She just kind of stared at me then. She couldn't very well say she wasn't, because we had one kid grown and married, and two more spoiled brats spending their father's money in college. Plus a special fund set aside by my wife's father, which has helped a whole lot, I admit.

She didn't like that Mother bit, but she was obviously pleased that I had agreed she could go to Spain with her friend Denise. I heard her talking to Denise later on the phone, and from what they said I realized their plans had gone a hell of a lot farther than her conversation that morning had suggested.

When she finished talking on the phone, I said, "Man Slays Spouse, Self."

"Would you drive us to the airport?" she said.

"Sure," I told her.

It was only three days later that she and Denise departed, which shows you how far along their planning had gone.

I went to the Rotary that day, after depositing the two girls at the airport in Columbus, which is sixty miles away, and then played golf all afternoon with Bix Bonham, Chester Farrell and Ed Pauly.

In Columbus I had bought a '69 Chevelle Malibu 2-dr. hardtop, V-8 engine, aut. transmission, and a '70 Ford Torino 2-dr. hardtop, V-8, gold finish with black vinyl roof, R&H, aut. transmission.

I paid good money for these babies, and they would certainly make nice little buys for two happy people.

Quality Pays.

5

About three o'clock on the afternoon of the day after my wife left, there was a good-looking young woman who came in to look for a VW. She had dyed blonde hair, was well built, and had a kind of surprised-looking face. Bucky was busy with a customer for a '66 Ford panel truck, and Cripps was over at the courthouse, doing some work on a title.

So I went up and began to talk to her. I was going along with the usual business about gas mileage, good rubber on the tires, low repair costs, and all that, when suddenly I looked up and, zap, this woman shot a look about three inches into my head. It was all the difference in the world.

I figure there are very few occasions when people *really* look at one another. One is if you think the other guy is trying to get fancy and put something over on you. Another is if you are just curious, and you are wondering what is going on in the other guy's head. So you look at him about three inches deeper than you usually do. And another time is if a man is interested in a woman, or vice versa.

The next thing I said, I was not thinking about it, but looking at her pretty much the same way, and that smile on her face was a little warmer, although it was still a little surprised-looking, a little zany.

Then she looked around a bit, and when I opened the door for her to sit behind the wheel, she eased in and brushed my arm with her breast. A natural thing to do, and it could happen any time a gentleman holds the door for a lady. And of course I help myself to an accidental touch or casual pinch every now and then, just to help the day along. But the fact was, I was thinking of more than selling a car by this time.

She looked around a little bit more, and she said she would think the deal over, and she left. Her name was Sheila Richards and she said she was a legal secretary for T. F. Hanaway, uptown. I had know T. F. for years, in Rotary and the country club, and I considered him a pretty decent old crook. Sheila Richards was maybe about thirty years old. No wedding ring.

Along about four-thirty, I went over to Yerby's for a double shot of Jack Daniel's, and I was thinking about several things, but mostly about Sheila Richards. I tried to analyze that look, and that soft brush of her breast against my arm. I thought about her: she had some mileage on her, but a lot of spirit, you could tell. She kept her eyes wide open, which gave her that surprised look. She had nice, rounded legs, faintly tanned. Her hair was fixed kind of nice. And she looked clean and warm and womanly. She was very neat the way she moved, like she was happy with herself, her little Secret, and everthing around her. She didn't even act very smart. She didn't know the first thing about cars, which is natural for a woman, but when I began to talk about different ways we could finance that nice little VW for her, she didn't seem to understand everything I was saying, and here she was supposed to be a legal secretary.

When I went back to the lot, it was a warm, balmy twilight. The air was as soft as a bubble bath. It was the kind of evening when you just might think of a Sheila Richards, even if you are old enough to know better.

Along about seven-thirty, Mr. Metzger walked in. When he came up to me, I said, "Alleged Rapist Pleads Guilty," and he nodded and said, "Hello, Mr. McCoy." Then he paused a second, and said, "What's that you were just saying?"

"Just a newspaper headline," I told him. "You know: a last-minute bulletin. Like 'Man, Woman Take Vows' and 'Senate Votes No on Appropriations.' "

He nodded and thought a second, and then he started bragging about how the Buick was doing. After a couple minutes of this, he told me he was going into the hospital in a few days to have his hemorrhoids operated on. He said this in a loud voice, and there was a family with three or four young kids only about thirty feet away. Cripps was showing a '69 Plymouth Sport Suburban to them. Automatic transmission and factory A/C.

I said that was too bad, but Mr. Metzger informed me that it wasn't so bad because it wasn't a major operation. Then he told me once more what a wonderful buy the Buick was, which I was getting sick and tired of hearing; and for a couple seconds I was afraid Metzger was going to go over to the family Cripps was waiting on and endorse McCoy's Car Sales as the best and most honest used-car business in the state.

Naturally, I was uneasy, but after a couple minutes of gab, the old windbag took off. It was then that I noticed Mother was in the old Buick, which he had parked out by the curb. She had just been sitting in there waiting while her husband was up in the lot talking.

Seeing her reminded me of the time a few days back when I had called my wife "Mother," and the surprised and thoughtful look she had given me.

It made me chuckle. Then I went back into the office and lit a panetela. It looked like Cripps might just sell that Plymouth, the way they were talking. I just sat there and puffed on the cigar and every now and then chuckled to myself. I couldn't help it.

I started reading one of my newspapers, but then I started thinking. After a few minutes, I got out a sheet of heavy glossy paper—almost like canvas—and laid it on the desk. I got out some heavy four-inch letter matrices and a bottle of bright-red paint. Then I made some lateral lines with a yardstick and pencil, and began to paint a sign.

Cripps came in after a while and said, "What is it this time, Rex?"

I told him to wait and see, and he got a Marlboro out of the cup on my desk and stood behind me, watching as I made the sign. This was the "Old Rex says" variety of sign.

After a while, Bucky came in, and he, too, watched me as I worked. Altogether it took only about twenty minutes, because I work fast on these signs, and enjoy it when there isn't a live customer on the lot.

When I finished it, I stood back and read it aloud for the boys, in case they were having trouble:

> OLD REX SAYS I WILL SELL YOU
> ANYTHING, INCLUDING MY CAR,
> MY FISHING ROD AND THE GOLD
> IN MY TEETH.

The two boys didn't say anything when I finished, so I picked it up in one hand and carried a chair in the other and went outside. I placed the chair in front of the signboard I have up—it has a little roof over it, with a couple of light bulbs underneath—and pinned up the new sign.

I like to make these signs myself, and I like to pin them up on this board, where everybody can see them. I bet I've made a thousand of them, every one of which I have thought up myself.

When I stepped down off that chair, there was a fellow named Clark Sissman waiting to buy a car from me. He didn't know it at the moment, but that's what he was doing.

He was looking over a '69 Pontiac Bonneville station wagon, six-way power seat, full vinyl interior and all the extras. I just let him circle for a few minutes, and then I threw out my lasso and had him tied and branded within an hour.

After this sale, I just kind of ambled around the lot and smoked a Dutch Masters or two, and kind of looked over my stock.

Then I began to think about Sheila Richards, and that crazy, wide-eyed, pretty face of hers.

Part of the problem with a Sheila Richards in a man's life, if he is a solid citizen of an old-fashioned community like ours, is where to take her, after he gets her warmed up and used to the idea.

I started thinking about this before I had had a chance to verify how serious the woman might be. I realized it could have been just the balmy spring weather, and the juice flowing high; or it could have been a cute little female trick to get the VW for a hundred dollars less than I was asking. She didn't have a trade-in.

The country club, the Episcopal church, Rotary . . . these are all part of the reason I had to be discreet. Part of the game, I figured, is if you have got to throw the traces, at least have the respect for the mores around you not to advertise what you are doing. In other words, you will always be forgiven provided nobody finds out you have something specific to be forgiven for.

I have had a few girl friends through the years, and I think my wife has probably suspected; but she's never said anything. Maybe she figures a man doesn't have the moral strength and dedication a woman would like him to have, and you really can't expect that the poor son of a bitch won't do a little occasional wandering beyond the lights.

I could imagine my wife finding out someday and

saying, "Well, so that's the one you threw me over for!" and I would explain, "I didn't throw you over, for Christ's sake. Birds Have Many Roosts, Only One Nest."

Then I could hear my wife saying, "You're a bird, all right!"

6

Three days had passed by, and I was figuring I might give Sheila Richards a ring on the telephone, when I looked outside and there she was, very much in the quivering, peaches-and-cream flesh, walking right up past that VW and headed straight for the office, with me in it.

Naturally, I went out and met her halfway, saying, "Never let a day pass without entertaining some vile thought."

She said, "What?"

"Never mind," I told her. "Sometimes I break out in a talking rash."

She kind of grinned and gave an interested look into each of my eyes.

"That certainly is an interesting sign up there," she said, looking at my handiwork.

"That isn't all I'll sell," I said. "There's also all my old merit badges."

"This is certainly some sale you're having, isn't it?" she said, looking all around with an admiring expression on her face.

"Woman Shoots Man Dead with Female Mannerisms."

"Honestly, I just don't know how you do it," she said, shaking her head with the wonder of it all.

"Do you like to fish?" I asked her. She gave me that look again. It was partly like I had said something to her in code, and she was taking an extra second or two to study me three inches behind the eyes and find out what I was really after.

"Or go boating?" I said. Then I thought of those sad-ass little rowboats and realized I'd have to talk her out of boating, if she said yes.

"Oh, yes," Sheila said, tickling the roof of the VW with her fingers. "I'm crazy about *anything* that has to do with the outdoors."

"I'll tell you what," I said. "Let's take this little beauty out for a spin."

Silence. Sheila staring at the roof of the VW where her two fingers are still resting, tickling it. Another couple seconds of silence. Then she turns her head and shoots me dead with another look, and I say, with my voice suddenly husky, "How about it?"

"Well," she says, which I of course know means yes. Yes to the suggestion about a spin; but also maybe yes to other questions that are still kind of whirling around in my mind like the lights on a roller coaster on a dark night.

So I put dealer's plates on the VW, hold the door while she climbs in (no breast brush this time, though I give her a chance), and in a couple seconds we were coasting out under the pennants of McCoy's Car Sales lot into the road and the sunshine and God knows what all.

"Why don't you drive out to Wingback Lake, and I'll show you the place," I said to her.

"Isn't that awfully far?" she asked, sounding kind of interested and happy. She was sitting right on the edge of the seat, holding the steering wheel like the reins of a horse, the way women always drive.

"Only about eight miles," I told her, giving her knee a tentative pat. I don't know why I said eight. It was eleven, as a matter of fact. The eight just came to me. Sometimes even *I* am surprised by what comes out of my mouth.

We drove along, making small talk. And everything was very cozy, because a VW is built for coziness, if you have a Sheila Richards at your side when it is a warm sunny day, and she is wearing a nice perfume and turning her head at about every traffic light to look at you and marvel at the wisdom of your words.

By the time we got to Metzger's, I had quoted a lower price to her, giving her a fifty-dollar cut. She thanked me, but still didn't accept the offer, which was not foremost in my mind at the moment, anyway.

We went up the road through the field, and suddenly there was the lake. An old couple sat fishing in one of the boats, about fifty yards from the dock. Only one car was parked there—a '67 light-tan Pontiac, R&H, I had sold personally to the old couple. They were named Potter, and he was a retired railroad man who collected stamps and liked to fish.

When Sheila pulled the car up behind some bushes, the Potters were out of sight, so I reached over and put my arm around her. Then something very strange happened: instead of turning around and zapping me with another look, she just stared straight ahead, right over the top of the steering wheel, with her eyes about half closed. A little as if somebody had just hit her in the stomach and knocked the wind out of her. And she didn't move.

I kissed her gently on the cheek, and she started humming very softly. But she didn't turn around. If by some strange chance the idea of the VW had come into my mind then, I might have given her the car.

But of course such an idea was far from my mind, as I suppose it was from hers, and with the Potters a hundred yards away from the dock (which I figured it would take the old fellow about ten minutes to row), I made my move. I reached up to turn Sheila's head around so that I could kiss her lips, but I jammed my thumb in her eye. It wasn't very hard, but she went "Ooooh," and asked me what I was trying to do. I didn't answer, but grabbed her face and kissed her good on the lips and then started caressing her heart breast. It was a nice handful.

As we were settling into a better position, I suddenly saw something move beyond the window in the corner of my vision, and when I pulled back I saw it was Mr. Metzger walking up to the car. The old fellow was looking hard at us as he approached, his head stuck forward and his hands shoved comfortably in the bib of his overalls, and one of his cheeks swollen with chewing tobacco.

I pulled back, and Sheila straightened her skirt out. I suggested that we drive away, and she quickly started the car and backed it around. Then she let the clutch out too fast, so that the car began to buck and bounce as we drove back the way we had come.

"Well," she said a few seconds later, when the car had settled down, "I *must* say!"

I didn't answer that, and we drove on a little farther, and then she said in a wobbly voice, "You certainly are quite a salesman, Mr. McCoy!" She was blinking a lot, I suppose from where I'd poked my damn clumsy thumb in her eye.

I made some sort of comment, but all I could think about was my last glimpse of old Metzger standing there with his hands still in his overalls and his one cheek bulged out and his eyes wide open with looking.

"Local Farmer Slain on Shore of Lake," I muttered, and Sheila didn't say anything.

7

I tried to remember when Metzger was supposed to go into the hospital for his operation. Sheila had cooed and ahed a lot when we had first driven up to Wingback Lake, and I realized that she was really big on this back-to-nature thing. It made me like her even more, in addition to her plump ass and other qualities. Because I am crazy about the outdoors, and always have been.

Also, the lake would be the safest place around. I had this deep, dumb suspicion that I couldn't possibly get into a motel within forty miles without the news making the networks on the late-evening TV shows or the morning headlines the next day.

It seemed to me that Metzger had said Thursday was the big day, but I wanted to be sure, so I called his house the next morning and asked for him.

It was a woman who answered, and I figured it was Mother. When I asked for Mr. Metzger, she said, "Is this Mr. McCoy?"

"Why, yes, Mrs. Metzger," I told her. "As a matter of fact, it is."

"Clendon isn't here, Mr. McCoy. Didn't he tell you this was the day he was going to the hospital?"

I answered that one of the reasons I had called was to check up on that very fact. And Mrs. Metzger said she was just about to go out of the house, because the operating room had been full earlier that morning and they had postponed the operation until eleven. So she had come home briefly, on an errand.

I told her to convey my best to the old bastard, and then

I hung up and called Sheila. I told her I would like to take her for another ride that evening.

She got a coy-but-kind-of-interested sound in her voice, and she said, "Where to?"

I told her I wanted to talk to her. I have found that when you tell a woman you want to talk to her, these are words so rich with implication and interest she is dazzled.

Sheila took a couple of breaths on the phone. I could hear her very clearly as she breathed, and then she said, "Where do you want to talk?"

"I thought we could take a drive. I would like to try out another cute little bug we have in stock, as a matter of fact, which I think we can give you a better deal on. Detroit Stunned by McCoy's Prices."

"What time?" she asked me, and I told her eight o'clock. By that time, I figured, it should be almost dark.

When I picked her up, she was dressed casually but wearing a kind of sparkly net over her hair, and I said to myself that Wingback Lake was going to be awfully nice this evening. If there were some fishermen there, with their heads filled with happy memories of the used-car deal they had gotten from Regius ("Rex") McCoy, the old Scotchman or Irishman or whatever I happened to be at the time of that particular campaign, I could park in the darkness and take Sheila up into the woods that surrounded the lake. I had thrown a thick blanket into the back seat, along with an unopened pint of blessed Jack Daniel's.

But as it was, the last two cars were departing as we drove in, and then we had the whole place to ourselves.

After we parked the VW, I picked up the blanket and the bottle, and we walked along the path beside the lake. A little farther on, the path turned away from the lake and went up about a hundred feet into a kind of meadow that was surrounded by woods. It was a fine spot.

As we walked, Sheila chatted nervously about herself.

She told me she was separated from her husband and didn't know exactly where he was, and she had a three-year-old girl living with her parents in Carlsbad, New Mexico. I spread the blanket out, and we sat down and kissed and took turns drinking from the pint of J. D. and looking at the new stars coming out.

Then things began to warm up exactly the way they should, and before too long Sheila's pretty silver panties were thrown aside and I was settling down to what I like to think of as pretty serious valve job and body work, when I saw a flashlight wavering on the path only about thirty feet below.

"Quick," I whispered, "there's somebody coming!" She raised her face, and I banged her cheek with my forehead as I squirmed around.

Shelia gasped and snatched up her panties and then sat on them. She pulled her dress down, and I jerked up my pants just as the flashlight flicked across us.

"Who is that?" a woman's voice asked.

Sheila hid her face, either from embarrassment or from where I'd bumped her, I couldn't tell which. While I was trying to think of something to say, the woman behind the flashlight said, "Why, it's Mr. McCoy, isn't it?"

Finally, after she asked the question again, I had enough sense to stand up and say, "Yes, as a matter of fact, it is. And who are you?"

But she was close enough now that I could see who it was. It was Mrs. Metzger. Mother herself.

"Clendon was worried about nobody around to watch the lake," she said in what seemed to be a tone of injury or betrayal.

"Send her away!" Sheila hissed. She was still holding her hands over her face. "Send her away."

"Is this *Mrs.* McCoy?" Mrs. Metzger asked. Apparently, she was hard of hearing.

"Yes, Mrs. Metzger," I said. "Everything's all right. You don't need to bother."

"Well, Clendon wanted me to keep an eye on things while he was in the hospital. He was so *worried* about not having anybody to watch the lake. You know. He *worries!*"

"Sure. That's just swell. I understand. Porpoises Found Music Lovers."

"I suppose you want to know how he's getting along?"

"Yes," I said. "How *is* he getting along?"

For an instant, I thought she was going to sit down for a long chat. I could see her kind of looking for a good place to sit, but since there wasn't any, and she'd never be able to get up off the ground by herself, she apparently decided against it. By now she had gathered enough sense to take the flashlight beam off of Sheila.

"Oh," she said, in the complaining tone of the elderly, "as good as can be expected, the doctor says."

"Well, that's fine," I told her.

"Mr. McCoy," the old woman said resentfully—as if I didn't deserve such devotion—"Clendon just thinks the *world* of you! Why, you just couldn't *believe* how much he likes that car. He's just crazy about it. I suppose Clendon told you we drove it to California, didn't he? San Francisco, Fresno, Santa Barbara, Los Angeles . . ."

Sheila suddenly got up, and walked off somewhere into the darkness of the woods.

Before I could say anything, Mrs. Metzger said, "Why, she walked off, didn't she? Where did she go?"

"Goddam if I know, Mrs. Metzger," I said through gritted teeth.

There was a shocked silence, until the old bat finally mumbled a few things about only trying to help out and then ambled off down the path.

I took a long drink and said, in a louder voice, "Woman Flees Moral Pursuer but Returns Safely."

I looked around for a while, and finally Sheila came out of the woods and said, "Take me home, please! And I certainly do hope I didn't get poison ivy."

I didn't say anything. The fact is, the whole hillside was lousy with poison ivy.

8

I thought about this fiasco, now and then, for a couple days, but I don't usually take things too hard. And so I didn't do anything except conjure up a few visions of Sheila Richards sitting in T. F. Hanaway's office, telling him everything that had gone on between us. Not that there had been much, in spite of all I could do.

I knew this was pretty fanciful, but the pictures kept coming back and filling my mind at odd moments. I got a long letter from my wife in London, her stopover on the way to Madrid. She wrote about four or five pages of description of things I couldn't care less about, and then, before the *"Hasta la vista,"* ended up by saying she was homesick and had never realized how much she loved me.

Well, she is a fine woman, and that letter warmed me up for a while, and I even hoped all the bruises on her soft white body (from my violent jerks and turns in my sleep, she tells me) would heal over there.

The weather was still fine, only a little too dry for the farmers. I strolled around the lot, smoking a Dutch Masters panetela that morning, patting the cars on their hoods, kicking a tire here and there (the hubcap came off a Corvair when I did that), and watching my boys, Bucky and Cripps, as they puttered about and screwed off.

Once I yelled out to Cripps, "Who's the best?" and he answered, "Rex is best!" and I gave him a big grin, free of charge.

It was the kind of day when you have to forgive the whole world, and I did exactly that. I thought of an old slogan I had used once: "If you're tired of wrecks, come to Rex!" I almost laughed out loud at the memory.

I love slogans! Son of a bitch, if I don't! Sometimes I'll even stop my car and study one alongside the road, if it hits me right.

I happened to notice a car that hadn't been washed yet. It was a '69 Dodge that I'd advertised as "aristocratic burgundy with black vinyl top, power brakes and steering, with torqueflite." I've always been crazy about the word "torqueflite." Once, I put it in an ad for a Buick—for the hell of it—and several customers pointed it out. I told them it was the newspaper that had made the error.

I yelled out to Cripps to have Rick or Willie come over and give the Dodge a good washing.

Cripps said he would, and then he said he was going to go get some coffee. He asked if I wanted a cup, and I told him no. He looked disappointed, because he knew if I'd said yes, I would have bought coffee for everybody. But I didn't.

Right after Cripps came back from having a cup of coffee at MacDonalds (this was about ten-twenty), I looked out the window and saw a man come wobbling towards me, lugging a heavy suitcase in one hand and a briefcase in the other. He was a funny-looking little duck, with long bushy sideburns and a big mustache spread out like a hairy butterfly all over his mouth. Also, one shoulder was about twice as wide as the other; it was like his head was put on off center. He was wearing a white short-sleeved shirt and a blue ascot scarf. His arms were no thicker than my wrists, and they were so hairy that they looked like they were covered with fur. He had a low, meaty forehead, with a deep, V-shaped wrinkle in it.

He looked sad and serious, and when I went out to meet him, he put down the suitcase and briefcase and just stood there a second, like he was giving me a chance to take him all in.

Finally I said, "Well, neighbor, what can I do for you this fine, good old American morning?"

"Are you Regius McCoy?" he asked.

"I'm the one," I said. "The one and only real McCoy. Found Living in Obscurity in Small Town. What can I do for you?"

"Dr. Winslow," he sighed, and then grabbed my hand and started shaking it up and down.

"What was that?" I said.

"Dr. Winslow. I wrote a letter to you a couple of weeks ago. I teach at the college."

"Oh, yes," I said. Then things started falling in place. His stationery had said, "Department of Psychology and Communications."

"You remember?" he asked.

"Sure," I said.

He dived down into his briefcase, brought out a folder, handed it to me and said, "Here is some information on what I'm doing."

I took it and laid it on my desk beside a sign I had printed, which says, "Living is Doing; and at McCoy's, Doing is SELLING."

Sometimes I put these little signs on my desk hoping to set a fire under the asbestos asses of Cripps and Bucky. I've got signs for my customers and signs for my salesmen. I fill the whole place with signs.

Anyway, I keep telling Bucky and Cripps there's no reason they can't sell more cars and make a little money for themselves. I kept beating my brains out trying to help the poor screwed-up, numb-ass bastards realize a few things, but they just don't seem to understand what I am saying.

"Aren't you going to read it?" Professor Winslow said.

"You mean right now?"

"No time like the present," he said.

I liked that, because "No time like the present" was exactly what I'd printed on one of those signs I just mentioned. That was a couple years ago, when Cripps, especially, was procrastinating in following up leads. I had a third salesman then, named Roger Colfax, but that is another story, and a long one.

Anyway, Professor Winslow was obviously waiting for me to read the folder, so I picked it up and read about the science of kinesics, which the folder explained was a study of "gesticulatory or nonverbal response communication."

"You understand what it's saying?" he asked, when I laid it back down on the desk.

"Sure," I told him, trying to drop the subject. I didn't particularly take to this bird.

"Don't let the gargling throw you," he said. "We're talking about the way people reveal themselves and tell you things by facial expressions, gestures, posture, and so on. The whole bit. My suitcase conceals a camera and sound track that will record customers as they listen to your sales talk. We'll confine ourselves to your customers alone, using you as a control factor. Of course, if you vary your technique in any way, that will be also part of the study. You know what I mean?"

"Sounds interesting," I said. "Show and tell. Or I guess it'd be tell and show."

"That's funny," he said, as if he were identifying an uncommon bird, or showing me how well he understood English.

"It was meant that way," I said. "Quips Liven Local Dealer's Day."

"And when we get all we need," he continued, "we'll abstract movement patterns from the hands, faces, eyes even, and other postural focal points so that we can study these movements in the abstract. We figure there should be as clear and dependable a vocabulary of gesture as there is of oral speech."

When he said that thing about a "clear and dependable" vocabulary, I suddenly thought of Miss Temple, who was a high-school teacher I had about thirty years ago, and I think she's still teaching. She's quite a woman in anybody's book. Miss Temple would swallow all the time, with her lips compressed, and say things like that. She was never more herself than just after she'd swallowed. Also, it seems to me those were the very words she used a number of times —a "clear and dependable" vocabulary.

Anyway, I told Professor Winslow to make himself at home, and he leaned over and thumped the suitcase with his knuckles, as if there were some bad-natured midget asleep in there, and he had to remind him it was time to wake up and go to work.

Just about all the time he had been talking, I noticed he wasn't looking at me. Right now, for example, I noticed he was looking at my right ear. "You were chosen very carefully," he said.

"Just call me Rex," I told him. "The Car Buyer's Friend."

"I can tell you there are people in this town who consider you a tremendous success at selling. The best around here, they say."

"I guess it's kind of an art," I said.

"I should say it is. But that doesn't mean there aren't aspects of this thing that can be understood more fully and communicated. You know what I mean? That's where I come in. My specialty, you might say, is the analysis of charisma."

I kind of nodded at that, but he had lied when he said I might have said it. Because I thought charisma just had to do with public speaking, and the ability to sway big groups of people to your own way of thinking. I was always kind of proud of my vocabulary, especially after having Miss Temple for a teacher, and I made a mental note to look this word up again and use it more often. I always kind of liked the sound of it.

Then I caught on to something as Professor Winslow was just standing there staring at me. It was just for a second, but what he was doing was looking about three inches inside my head, with that particular look you don't see very often, as I've said before.

"I have a theory," he said, looking back at my ear once again, "that charisma is not limited in its effects to large crowds or groups of people. I have a theory that it is very much an operative, generally unacknowledged but somewhat measurable factor in interpersonal relationships."

"Is that right?" I said.

"And from what I've heard, I'd say that you had some of this quality. It's what makes you a good salesman; it's that simple."

As he talked, he took out a pipe and lit it. Then he turned the bowl upside down and started puffing away between words. Because I already could see that this hairy little duck was a talker, I kind of put what he was saying out of my mind. I also forgot about that look he had sunk behind my eyes, not realizing how important a bit of evidence this could prove to be in the light of later events.

"Well," I said, walking away and waving my hand, "just make yourself at home. Car Tycoon Welcomes Visitors to Lot."

Suddenly I heard a hoarse falsetto voice say, "Who's 'at, Rex?"

I turned around, and there was Buckholz leaning against the VW that Sheila was interested in buying. As usual, his pants legs were pulled halfway up his calves, and he was squinting in the sun. A toothpick was in his mouth. The inside part of his tie had blown into his pocket, and his shirt was damp and wrinkled from sweat.

"Thousands Suffer from Baldness," I said.

But old Bucky wasn't going to be put off, and he repeated the question, so I answered it. "That was some professor," I said. "He wants to measure the way people react to my sales talk."

Bucky pulled violently at his crotch. "He *what?*" he said.

"Never mind," I told him. "I'll tell you later. Just don't tell anybody what he's doing."

"Hell, I won't tell nobody," Bucky said, standing up straight so suddenly it made the VW lurch. "Because I don't know what he's doing my *own* self."

I turned away and went over to check out a '69 Plymouth we had just taken in. Boy Can Be Taken Out of Country, I was thinking, but goddam if Country Can Be Taken Out of Boy.

9

Later, things were pretty slow, and I happened to look at this little cup I have on the desk for cigarettes, and saw that there were only about four left. I rummaged around in the drawer, but there weren't any more packs, so I called Cripps in and gave him a five-dollar bill.

"Why don't you test drive that Mercury," I told him,

"and while you're out, stop in someplace and get a carton of Marlboros."

Cripps said sure, and went out to a '68 Mercury we had just taken in.

I keep this cup full of cigarettes for customers mostly, but for Cripps, too. Bucky doesn't smoke, and sometimes I see him stare longingly at that cup full of fresh cigarettes, as if he is almost ready to take up the habit just so he can free-load on me.

Cripps is always digging into the cup, but I don't mind. I want these two boys of mine to be happy and relaxed here. As much as I love to sell, I don't want to sell with dis-gruntled salesmen. I don't suppose I spend over four or five bucks a month on cigarettes, and even if Cripps does get more than his share, four or five bucks isn't going to hurt me, when I sell more cars without trying than Bucky and Cripps do together. In a way, it isn't fair that selling should be so much fun and come so easy to me, and be so grim and irrelevant and hard for them, but that's the way it is.

Along about one o'clock, Cripps returned with the car-ton of Marlboros and said he was sick at his stomach.

"I'm going home and take some paregoric," he said. His bad eye was really wild.

"Sure, go ahead," I told him. "If that Thompson kid comes in, I'll go ahead and close for you."

"Thanks," Cripps said. But then he just stood there for a couple seconds, staring out the window with his hands in his pockets.

I was looking at the latest issue of *Outdoor Life,* and I was kind of wishing Cripps would get the hell gone if he was going to go.

Then I heard Professor Winslow, who had stationed himself in the office, start to tap his pipe out against the window sill, and say, "You allergic to something, maybe?"

"No," Cripps said. "Why?"

"Why? Because everybody knows that's one of the things that can cause intestinal upset. My problem is headaches."

Cripps just shook his head and looked glumly at nothing. When he felt bad, which was pretty frequent, his eyes looked more crooked than usual. It was like he had lost a little of the power to focus them.

"Are you a doctor?" Cripps asked him a couple seconds later.

Professor Winslow blew through the stem of his pipe. "Not an M.D., if that's what you mean."

"I just wondered," Cripps said. "I'm going. Good-by."

"So long," I said. Winslow waved good-by with his pipe, but Cripps didn't look around. He also forgot to give me back change from that five.

I asked Winslow if he'd gotten some good pictures this morning.

"I got one good shot of that farmer with the cowboy hat. I can do something with that."

"You're kind of wasting your time, it looks like," I said.

Winslow shrugged and stuffed the pipe in his pocket. "No. I been getting some study in."

Then a kid of about twenty came in. It was Cripps's customer, who worked in a filling station. His name was Harold Thompson, but everybody called him Bo.

I went out to wait on him, and about fifteen minutes later I had closed the deal for Cripps. I was wondering if Winslow had been grinding away with the camera and tape recorder. When I finished with the Thompson boy, I returned to the office. After a few minutes, Winslow scraped his chair back and pointed at my *Outdoor Life*. "Don't tell me you like that sort of thing," he said. "The great outdoors!"

"I guess I'll plead guilty," I said. I turned around

and pointed to the rack of elk antlers hanging on the back wall, right next to the ceiling.

"See that?" I said. "I killed that old fellow eleven years ago, in British Columbia. Got him with one shot at about a hundred and twenty yards, 30-06, 220 grain spitzer point."

"Very impressive," Winslow said. But he didn't sound impressed; he sounded like he personally resented me being interested in something he wasn't interested in.

About fifteen minutes later, Bucky came in and said, "Well, how's it going?" He is always asking this. About every hour.

"Okay," I told him, and threw the *Outdoor Life* on the desk.

Bucky nodded. He was chewing a toothpick and staring at Professor Winslow, who was reading and puffing on his pipe.

"Rough day," Bucky said after a bit. Then he heaved a big sigh. He always acts like a man who is fatigued from hard manual labor, but what he meant by rough day, I guess, was that he hadn't sold anything or gotten a good prospect or heard any recent ball scores.

A couple minutes later, the phone rang. It was a woman from Milford who had been trying to finance a '69 Toronado. She asked me a lot of questions, and then she asked me to hold on a minute while she looked for a list of questions Ted Wilshire, of the Savings and Loan, had given her to ask. I could have told her every question, along with the answers, but I knew she was a little bit wary, so I let her go and look.

While I was waiting there on the phone, I saw that Professor Winslow had put his book down and was staring at Bucky.

Then he leaned forward towards Bucky and said, "Tell me about yourself."

"What?"

"Tell me about yourself. How do you manage to keep sane in a place like this?"

Bucky almost dropped the toothpick out of his mouth.

"You talking to me?" he said.

"Sure," Professor Winslow said. "Tell me about how you stand up under it, being a salesman here in the boondocks?"

Bucky just stared at him for a few seconds, and then he mumbled something and walked out the door.

Professor Winslow looked at me and said, "Very defensive, isn't he?"

But before I could answer, the woman from Milford was back on the phone, asking if the Toronado had automatic steering. I said she probably meant power steering, and yes, it did. And then we talked for another five minutes before the poor rattled old bag hung up.

About a half hour later, I was out on the lot, and Bucky came up to me and said, "What in the hell is he trying to get out of me?"

"Bucky," I said, "he's probably just interested in people, since he's a psychologist. That's all. He probably didn't mean anything."

"I'll bet," Bucky said. He gave a tug at his crotch and grunted. " 'Tell me about yourself!' Shee-yut!"

Just then a couple of men came into the lot, and I told Bucky to go over there and buckle down and sell them a car. And make himself a couple hundred. Bucky gave one more tug at his crotch, pulled the end of his tie out of his shirt pocket, and took off.

When I turned around, I saw Rick Ruggles and Willie Byrd walking up on the lot, so I waved to them and they waved back. They work in the Shell station about fifty yards up the street, and I hire them to wash our stock. Rick Ruggles is a quiet kid with a bad complexion, and Willie Byrd is a colored fellow who stutters. He only stutters on one letter though, I've noticed, and that is the letter *h* when it begins a word. I've also noticed that for some goddam reason he seems to go out of his way to use words that begin with *h*.

These are a couple of pretty nice kids, and they like to come over a lot and shoot the bull with us when things are slow at the Shell station. I suppose it sounds conceited, but the truth is they say they like to hear me talk.

Sometimes I give one of them a buck and send him out for ice-cream cones or milkshakes at the Dairy Freeze, which is about half a mile away. Usually, Rick goes, and Willie stays at the station or here at the lot.

Today I don't give them a buck, and they don't care, because they really just like to come over and talk with Bucky or Cripps, like I say. Or hear me tell a story now and then.

But I don't feel like talking right now, so they hang around Bucky, after he predictably fumbles a sale with the two men from out of town, and I just stand there quietly, with my hands in my pockets, and look out over my lot and kind of analyze the stock I have on hand.

The three of them are over there talking, Bucky leaning against a new Ford Country Squire wagon, and Rick Ruggles and Willie Byrd standing in front of him, like two sparrows in front of a corn-fed bull.

So finally I go over to kind of tune in on what they are saying, and Bucky looks up and says, "Who was it you sold that car to last week, Rex? You know, the lawyer from Milford."

"Bucky," I said very slowly, "there are no cars."

"What?" he said.

"Just what I said: there are no cars. Like I've told you and Cripps a thousand times. There are '70 Mustangs and '65 Corvairs, and there are '66 Toronados and '68 Vista Cruisers. But there are no cars."

Bucky looked like I had slapped his face in front of

friends, so I tried to make things easier by grinning and showing all my gold teeth. Also, I got out a Dutch Masters panetela and chuckled a little louder than was strictly spontaneous.

"What's he talking about, Bucky?" Rick Ruggles asked.

"I know what h-h-h-he trying to say," Willie Byrd said. "H-h-he trying to say: don't say cars, say Mustang and Corvair."

"Willie Byrd is absolutely correct," I said, blowing cigar smoke over his head. "And if you boys ever want to be salesmen, remember to use brand names all the time. It's a way of being specific."

"Hell, *I* don't know what kind of car you sold that lawyer, Mac," Bucky said, standing up. He started to reach for his crotch for a friendly tug, but apparently decided it would be too undignified under the circumstances.

"Bucky," I said, planting my feet hard on the ground in preparation for a lie, "you are a good salesman, and it isn't like you to forget an important detail like that. Cars are our bread and butter, and nobody knows that fact better than Buckholz."

That kind of embarrassed him, and he said, "Hell, I don't exactly know about that."

"And that's why I am so surprised you would forget an important detail, such as what kind of car it was I sold to Mr. Detwiler, the attorney from Milford. But to answer your question, it was a '69 Oldsmobile, a V-8 Cutlass. Factory A/C, R&H. Melody lemon with white sidewalls."

"Hell, if it was my own sale, I would of remembered," Bucky said.

"I know you would, Bucky," I said, lying again, because I hadn't really meant to embarrass him in front of Rick and Willie. "But you know, I always like to make this point about trade names: they distinguish one thing from another, and they establish character and individuality. Do you see what I mean, fellows? This may sound a little fantastic to you, when I put it to you this way, but I want to suggest to you that, by God, this is simply one humble, little, unnoticed instance of the way conformity and a brainless socialistic homogenizing influence is working its way into our lives. I mean, when we reduce all Galaxies and T-Birds, all Impalas and Electras, to a single, indiscriminate word, 'car,' we have, by God, lost our ability to make important distinctions, and what—I would like to ask you—is the mind for, if not to make important distinctions?"

Goddam, if I wasn't really getting wound up; old Bucky and Rick Ruggles and Willie Byrd just kind of simultaneously let their mouths ease open, and I was so caught up in their vulnerability to what I was saying that I got even more eloquent, and started punching my right index finger into my left palm. This is usually where the actual sale starts to happen, I have noticed.

"Think of how colorless this world would be if we didn't distinguish one brand of something from another, each brand busting its ass trying to outproduce, outinvent, outdo and outsell the other! Hell, we would be living in a world of things, that's all. I mean, if you're going to call all cars just cars, why in the hell don't we start including tractors and trucks in the same word? And then, pretty soon we're calling sewing machines and ball-point pens by the same name. Refusing to discriminate, see? Without discriminating, what is the mind to do?"

"I don't see h-h-how discrimination is good," Willie Byrd said.

I turned to him and saw what he meant, and I said, "Goddammit, Willie, I didn't mean that kind of discrimination. I meant the kind that refuses to distinguish between a Plymouth and a Rambler, for Christ's sake."

"You mean 'distinction' then," Willie said.

"No, goddammit, I mean 'discrimination,' because 'distinction' often has the connotation that something is distinct because it's good, and I'm not saying Plymouths and Ramblers are all that good. What I mean is . . ."

"But you *said* 'distinction' earlier, didn't you?"

"By God, I did at that, but that was a different context. Still, you can use the word 'distinction' if the context is right."

"Jesus Christ Almighty," Bucky said, turning around in a circle, "let me come up for air."

Rick Ruggles laughed a little, and Willie Byrd doubled over leisurely in a silent guffaw.

I laughed, too, because it had gotten to be a pretty screwy lecture, especially for somebody like Bucky, who is convinced that all subtlety should be reserved for football and baseball, the latter especially.

"It's still true, though," I said. "As I was trying to point out before Willie here got me off track: if you push this thing to the logical extreme, then you'll start calling everything a 'thing,' because that includes everything, and that's as far as you can push the common denominator."

"Whatever you said, Mac," Bucky said, "I agree with you." Willie Byrd laughed and said, "Me, too. Man, you could talk a cow through a buttonhole."

"The old Mac can talk, all right," Bucky said admiringly. "He's the world's number one champion."

Well, I puffed on my Dutch Masters panetela and kind of ambled away, bumping into Willie Byrd when I turned around. I was sorry as hell I had busted in on their conversation. Something didn't taste right. Part of the thing that went wrong was that I didn't really feel like talking to anybody, as I have said. It was strange.

My leg had been hurting, too.

When I was far enough away from them so they couldn't hear, I said, "Local Man Plays Tricks on Self."

By this time, my leg was really beginning to hurt.

10

Late that afternoon I was reading the Dayton *Daily News,* and I happened to look up, and who should I see but Harley Grumbacher, the editor of our local newspaper. He was standing there letting about a bushel of belly hang out in front of a nice little Corvette, slapping some papers against his thigh and puffing on an R. G. Dun.

I went up to him and said, "Well, Harley, Local Newsman May Purchase Car."

Harley looked up at me and said, "Hello, Rex. I see you're still in competition with us. Why don't you lay off the headlines, and I'll promise not to sell cars."

"Innocent Man Pleads Guilty," I said, "but Rejects Scribe's Deal."

Harley just kind of nodded and gave me the once-over with his eyes, which are very puffed and sleepy-looking. He has an expression on his face like that of a man who has swallowed all the bad news of a lifetime, and isn't even curious any longer. Harley is a little more lively than this, however; I've played poker with him now and then, and he can be a real alert son of a bitch upon occasion.

I asked Harley if he was interested in a car, and he said no, his wife just had to do a little shopping and he thought he'd drop by to see what I had gotten in the lot recently.

"I'm always getting fresh stock," I said. "The way I figure it, Harley, I pay a few bucks more than the other fellow and sell for a few dollars less. That way, we all profit. According to my philosophy, this is what life's all about."

I went on like this for a few minutes, and pretty soon old Harley's eyes got a strange little glint in them, and I knew damned well I could have sold him something right then and there, but I let up on him after a bit and watched him walk away. I do this now and then, the way you sometimes catch a small bass, or maybe even a big one like Harley, and put him back in the water. It's the sport that matters, not the money.

It was strange. I know why Harley came by to see me: he wanted to hear me talk, hear me tell him about my cars. *He* may not have realized this was the reason, but I did.

The poor overworked and worried bastard doesn't have the first ounce of respect for me, but I can twist him around my finger. I say this without conceit. It is the simple truth. He is too caught up in the confusion of the world to understand it.

And he comes by to hear me talk, for he knows I have conviction, and he can feel the power, by God.

It is a little game we play with each other. He drops by every now and then, and feels pleased because he has never fallen for my sales talk . . . or so he thinks, because he has never bought a car from me.

But I know better.

When Harley left, I went back in my office and made a sign that said:

COME IN AND SHAKE MY HAND
AND LOOK ME IN THE EYE;
AND EVEN IF THERE'S NOT A SALE,
I'LL SMILE AS YOU GO BUY.

By now it was almost four-thirty, so I decided to go over to Yerby's for a drink, and on an impulse I asked Professor Winslow if he wanted to go.

He frowned and sighed. Then he shrugged and said, "Why not?"

"What do your friends call you?" I said.

"What makes you think I have any friends?" he asked.

"Cut out the crap," I said.

"All right," he said. "My name happens to be—and I'm not shitting you one iota—Homer Winslow. Can you believe it?"

I didn't know what he was getting at, but the fact didn't bother me. "Sure I believe it," I said. "What does it cost?"

"Actually, everybody calls me Jerry," he said.

"Fine," I said. I was sorry I had brought the whole matter up, and sorry I had invited him to come have a drink with me.

"If they call me anything, that is," he said.

"What?"

He closed his eyes. "Look, forget it. Never mind. Okay?"

"Sure. My view exactly. And as long as we're on the subject, call me Mac. Or Rex. Or even Regius, which is my real name, as a matter of fact. Call me whatever you want. I am adaptable. Local Dealer Known by Many Names."

When we went into Yerby's I ordered a Jack Daniel's from Bonnie, and Winslow frowned a little (that V in his forehead getting so deep you could have stuck a dime in it and it wouldn't have fallen out), and then he asked what kinds of wine they had.

"We got all kinds," Bonnie said, easing forward and leaning her pelvis against the table. She always acts tired, like she's got a broken back.

Winslow closed his eyes and nodded. "I'll have a glass of sherry.

"If she knows what sherry is," he said, after she left. He crossed his eyes and went, "Duhhhh," and then lolled his tongue around like an idiot.

"She might know," I said. She returned with the drinks, and Winslow started talking and gesturing as if before a large crowd he had to convince of something. He started telling me about his work, a lot of which was boring and technical, so I started thinking of my wife. I thought of her at her stopover in London, standing beside one of the Regimental Guards with their big bearskin hats. Maybe I thought of this because of Winslow's hair, because it stuck out like a big shaggy fur cap.

It occurred to me that with her bizarre tastes, she might even be impressed by this bird, and listen to every word he said. I sighed, finished off the J. D., and asked him if he was ready for another glass of wine.

"I've hardly touched this one," he said. So I ordered another J. D. and lighted a Dutch Masters.

Then Winslow studied me a minute as I puffed on the cigar, and finally he said, "Rex, tell me about yourself. You lived in this ass-hole town all your life?"

I managed to keep a straight face and handled the question a little better than Bucky had. Still, after I had talked for about five minutes, it occurred to me that I hadn't said much.

But he apparently thought otherwise. He pointed his finger at me as if I had been judged and convicted. "You're very interesting," he said. "In ways you probably don't even realize."

"What do you mean by that?" I asked him.

"That, I can answer in one word," he said. "Charisma. You know something?"

I shook my head no.

"They think I'm nuts about this thing. What does a professor at some little goddam college in the fucking boondocks know? Half of them think I'm defining the obvious, and the other half think what I'm doing all adds up to about fifteen tons of bullshit. But what do those ass holes know? But I'll tell you something," he said, jabbing the table with his index finger, "without going too far—which would be stupid at this point—I'll tell you this: you're a living example of what I'm talking about."

I didn't know what to say to that, so I kept quiet and nodded. Right then, I remembered that several times that afternoon I had sensed that this fellow was over there watching me. Not just when I was operating on a customer (after all, that was what he *said* he was there for), but even when I was licking my thumb and turning a page of the *Outdoor Life,* or reading a newspaper, or leaning back in my creaky chair and surveying my domain, with my hands clasped behind my head, or pulling the drawer all the way out of my desk, and spilling all the contents on the floor (as I'm always doing), or lighting up a panetela, or whatever in the hell else I do when I am not doing anything in particular. He had a way of watching a man very close, I could tell.

He nodded. "A living example," he said.

"Well, that's very interesting," I said. "Two Flee Police in Stolen Cars."

"Believe me, it's more than interesting. It's remarkable."

"It is?"

"More than that," he said, getting wound up. "It's extraordinary."

For a couple seconds, then, Professor Winslow sank his stare about three inches into my head. Then his lips twitched once, like he was kissing the air, while he was still looking at me that way; and then he pinched the bridge of his nose with his thumb and forefinger.

"What's the matter?" I asked him.

"Nothing. I get fucking headaches is all. Spasms."

"You got one now?"

"You learn to live with them. Believe me, they're nothing. If they were something, I'd have them taken care of. Right?"

I looked over his shoulder and saw Yerby standing by the jukebox, scratching his ass in a studious sort of way and looking kind of unfocused.

"Believe me," the professor said, taking his hand down from his head. "You have extraordinary gifts."

"I've often wondered if it isn't kind of like ESP," I said.

He nodded. "A connection, maybe, but I personally don't think so. What do they *know* about ESP? Nothing."

I finished my double, and then we both had beef sandwiches, being the least of a whole menu of evils available from Yerby. All the time we ate, Winslow was talking.

11

When we finished eating, we went back to the lot. Winslow had parked his car on the street in front, and he piled his equipment in and said good-by.

This was not an evening when we stayed open late, so I closed up—which took me about fifteen or twenty minutes—and when I went out to get into my Buick, I saw that Winslow's car was still there, with its hood raised, and the professor with his head stuck underneath.

I walked up and asked him what was wrong.

He pulled his head out and said, "The goddam thing won't budge."

"What seems to be the trouble?" I asked.

He laughed mirthlessly. "You're asking *me* what the *trouble* is?"

"That was the impression I got. I think that's what I asked."

"Listen, I don't know shit about a car. Didn't *ever* know shit about a car, and don't even intend to *learn* shit about a car."

"Millions Flee Homes in Giant Quake."

"It just doesn't want to start," he said.

"Did it turn over?"

"What's 'turn over'? Look, where I come from, we want to go somewhere, we take a taxi. Right? I leave this shit to the grease monkeys."

"Local Dealer Tells Professor to Fuck Self."

He took his pipe out of his pocket and put it upside down in his mouth and said, "Just leave the fucking thing. I'll have a man from the filling station come get it tomorrow."

"It'll be all right on the street," I said.

"Listen, do you go past the college on your way home?"

"No," I said, "but come on and get in. I'm leaving now, and I'll drop you off."

He nodded seriously, and we piled his things in the back seat of my Buick.

We drove silently up the main street of town toward the college. I saw Sheila Richards walk out of a drugstore, and I honked and pulled over to the curb, where there happened to be two empty parking spots. I pressed the electric button to lower the window on Winslow's side, and leaned across to speak to her.

"Local Dealer Has Fantastic Bargains," I said.

For a second she didn't seem to know who was in the car (seeing Winslow's furry head would throw a lot of people off), and she just looked kind of pretty and uncertain there on the sidewalk. But when I spoke, she smiled and said, "Oh, I just bet you do!"

It was nice and flirty, the way she said that, and I asked if she wanted a ride anyplace, but she said no, she had to meet her roommate to go to a wedding shower of a very close friend.

So we buzzed away, and Winslow said, "Who's the cute pussy?"

"That young lady," I said, "is a prospective customer."

When we got to the campus, I drove around to the back of Taylor Hall, which is where Winslow said his office was. I told him about my going to college there, and playing football, and being all-conference guard one year, way back when they had the single wing.

"Listen," Winslow said. "I'll just be here a minute to put this equipment away, and then you can drop me off at my house. I'll buy you some gas sometime."

"Forget it," I said. "And take your time. I'm not in any hurry."

"No point in waiting out here," he said. "Come on in, and I'll show you my office."

So I carried his suitcase in, while he led the way and unlocked the door of Taylor Hall and switched on the lights. It is an old building, dating from 1910 or so, and the ceilings are about twenty feet high on the first floor.

Winslow's office was down the first hall of the first floor; he pitty-patted ahead of me and opened the door.

After he switched on the lights of his office, the first thing he did was show me pictures of his wife and three boys, and then he talked a little about several of the paintings on the walls, which were by members of the art department. They looked pretty goddam goofy to me, but I didn't say anything. After a while, they didn't look quite so bad, just because this screwball was so enthusiastic about them. As I've mentioned, I'm vulnerable to enthusiasm, because I've got selling in my blood.

The more he talked, the more you could tell he really liked his office. A little bit the way I like my old converted two-car garage. He showed me some charts and things, and stuck a book in my hand he said he wanted me to borrow and read.

Finally I told him, "Prominent Car Dealer Has to Take Piss," and he said go ahead, that he had to write a short note to his student assistant, and he'd be through in a minute.

So I walked down the hallway to the men's room. I went inside, flipped on the light switch, and stood there for a minute looking at this old son of a bitch in the mirror. It was hard to believe this was a reflection of me, the real McCoy. The man in the mirror was wearing a soft, light, pale-gray shirt with a black string tie. He was totally bald in front. He had a red and suntanned whiskey face that was wrinkled and kind of square, and his puffy eyes were what you might term crafty.

I went over to the fourth urinal and unzipped. While I was standing there, I looked over the pictures and inscriptions etched in pencil and ball point for the edification of idle scholars at such moments as this.

One of them almost stopped my water for good. It said, "Sheila Richards Fucks." That was all. Crudely etched there at eye height, for every Taylor Hall customer to contemplate. When I was zipping up, Winslow came in, his bushy head and face almost emitting sparks; and he started blowing out tired sighs like a horse when he went over to one of the washbasins and began washing his hands and face.

When he finished, he vibrated his hands like a mad pianist and reached for a towel. I flicked a cigar ash on the tile floor, and he said, "Tell me about your family." He unzipped and aimed himself at Sheila Richards' urinal.

So I told him about my boy and my two daughters. By the time I'd finished, we were outside on the campus. It was a warm, sweet evening, and it was nice the way the lamp posts lining the campus walk shone through the trees.

Suddenly Winslow stopped and took a deep breath. Apparently he had been noticing how nice it was, too, because he said, "All this is unreal. Never-Never Land. Peter Pan and Wendy. You know what I mean?"

"It looks real to me," I said.

"No, that's not what I mean. I mean you people are escapists, out here in your little world. All the shitheads teaching here in their little ivy-covered tower, and you with your corny newspaper headlines and your hot deals and your used cars. While half the world's starving and in turmoil, and people everywhere are trying to bring about a new world . . . you stay here in this little imitation world of yours and ignore the real things happening."

I was so surprised, I didn't even get mad, although I did have a brief fantasy of grabbing him by his butterfly mustache and throwing him about twenty yards.

But all I said was, "I don't see how one place is any more real than another."

"That isn't what I mean!" Winslow cried, raising his hands and grabbing fistfuls of air. "Can't you feel it? Don't you read what's happening? I'm talking about the revolution, man—the Blacks in the big cities and the war and the transformation of all the old ways. As sweet and nice as all this is"—he waved his hand at the campus—"it's irrelevant now. This isn't where we're going to live any longer. I'm speaking of mankind. It's about time you people realized that."

I didn't answer, because it occurred to me that Professor Winslow just might be composed of undiluted, one-hundred-per-cent, government-inspected bullshit.

I dropped him off at his house and then started to drive home. I thought about stopping at Yerby's for a nightcap, but for a change I decided I didn't really want one.

When I got home, I looked up the word "charisma" in my wife's big new unabridged dictionary. I call it hers because she insisted on getting it. It's a handsome book, and it lies open on a stand in what my wife calls the library. Where it would just gather dust, as far as I can see, except for the occasions when I look something up in it. Usually I use a smaller dictionary on the night stand in our bedroom if I want to look something up.

When I finished, I closed the dictionary, and one of my wife's four Angora cats rubbed its side against my bare ankles. I was wearing just boxer shorts, and beyond the windows, in the distance, I could see the network of lights in the car lot, and, far beyond that, I could see the college dome, which was next to Taylor Hall, where old fucked-up Professor Homer Winslow busied himself at charts and graphs and books and students, and where Sheila Richards' name resided in modest and quiet eloquence above the fourth urinal.

Somewhere to the right stood a small office building, where T. F. Hanaway held forth at the law, utilizing the services of this good-looking secretary, with a lot of hard mileage but probably still sound in the springs, whose womanly treasure was once briefly assaulted by a local character, the flamboyant but aging owner and proprietor of McCoy's Used-Car Sales.

Which man, in turn, Professor Winslow had claimed, was extraordinarily endowed with charisma: "A unique personal power conceived of as belonging to those exceptional individuals capable of securing the allegiance of large numbers of people."

Winslow had led me to believe I had more of this than practically any goddam body around.

Local Man Found to Have Unique Personal Power.

Son of a bitch! I kind of liked the sound of it.

12

The next morning I had a kind of furry head and an uncertain stomach, even though I had only drunk a couple of nightcaps before going to bed.

Things were quiet, so I got to work on a big sign that said:

I WANT TO SELL TO YOU
I WANT TO BUY FROM YOU.
THIS IS CALLED GIVE AND TAKE,
AND IT HAPPENS TO BE WHAT LIFE
IS ALL ABOUT, MY FRIEND.

It was one of the longest signs I had ever made, and I was hoping I could get all the words on without making them look too cramped.

Winslow came in and watched me for a while. I heard him sucking on his upside-down pipe as he stood behind me. Then he went over to his place by the window and began to work on something.

It was that morning that I think I first fully realized there was something up I didn't know about. Occasionally I would catch him sitting there, holding his place in the book with his finger, and just watching me. Other times he ignored me too completely, and pretended not to hear me if I asked him a question. He had something up his sleeve.

But it wasn't just him. Cripps was still feeling bilious,

and Buckholz started right in talking about baseball. Like a lot of fat men, Bucky thinks the only serious thing that happens in the world is sports. This is the only subject that even brings him near the precincts of higher thought. I think the son of a bitch came to work for me only because he is a local boy (he was raised on a farm about six miles out), and he was at an impressionable age when I made college all-conference as strong-side guard.

Now he can't get over the fact that I don't even follow the goddam sport. Football, I mean; and baseball is even less to me. Bucky has a wife and four kids, but he'd sell them all on the auction block to see the Redlegs play Philadelphia or the San Francisco Giants in a double-header.

Well, he starts in this morning, and I just kind of sit there and watch the sun get blacker, until a couple of boys come in to look at a reconditioned '69 Thunderbird we've had in stock for over two months.

Cripps was showing a pale-gray '70 Chrysler Newport to two men I didn't know, so Bucky had to leave the happy world of batting averages for a few minutes, and I was able to draw a few breaths and meditate. Winslow was deep in his book, presumably waiting for the time when I might go into action.

For a while, all I could think about was that sentence somebody had written above the urinal. To tell the truth, I had been about to call Sheila again and tell her I had even a better deal than before. She'd know I was talking in code, and she'd know that I knew it, too. There are some things you just don't come out and say.

But of course now, after I had seen her name above the urinal, I didn't know what to do. I hoped the information was true, but naturally I didn't want it to be *too* true, and I didn't want it to be too public.

These thoughts made me feel all the worse. I was despondent also because this was the first day of June. That meant that the May sales campaign was officially over. It had been a hell of a success in total sales; but the fact was I had accounted for a greater volume than Cripps and Buckholz together. It was always this way. And not because I hogged the sales, because I never did that. After all, this is my business, and I want to keep my salesmen happy. I almost always let Bucky and Cripps take the first customers. But no matter what sales ideas I get, I seem to come out way the hell ahead.

I suppose it's my charisma. I love to talk to people, most of the time, and get them to see my way of thinking. Sometimes their eyes kind of glaze over, the way some people get when they're deeply affected by music. I never look three inches inside their heads at moments like this; I never look at them at all. I just kind of focus a half-inch in front of the bridge of their nose and give way to my own voice. I figure this is for the same reason that a surgeon doesn't want to know about a patient's love life, or a lawyer doesn't want to know about a client's dreams.

To operate on people you have to maintain a certain distance.

Part of my despondency right now had to do with feeling kind of crummy about outselling old Bucky and Cripps.

Also, the simple, undeniable part is, I like to *do* things and *build* things and, goddammit, *create*. I always have. And I have always liked to sell cars, but I also like to be successful at anything, whether it has to do with cars or not. And now that the Wingback Lake campaign had ended, I felt kind of empty. Not only that, I had jockeyed myself out of at least one pretty decent place to catch bass.

I stared out the front window at Cripps and Buckholz, and listened to Professor Winslow blowing bubbles through his upside-down pipe, along with an occasional cloud of Sir Walter Raleigh. Now and then I thought of

Sheila's debut on the shithouse wall in Taylor Hall, and I was about ready to leave and get out on the water. This was a weekday, and I knew a little stream on the back road to Milford where *no* goddam body ever fished. It looked like a good place for bass. I would get a six-pack of Miller High Life, pack the cans in ice down in my portable, lightweight cooler, then get out my Heddon Pal, Mark II, 6½-foot Flex Action rod, and I would climb in my car and go out and fish, by God.

Then Professor Sad-ass cleared his throat at me and said, "You're happy doing this sort of thing? Selling is all? Selling is *it?*"

I told him sure, I was happy.

He shook his head sadly. "Me," he said, "I couldn't stomach it. Not for a fucking minute. Most of the time I feel too goddam irrelevant as it is, out here in the middle of Nowheresville."

I didn't say anything to that, and then after a long breath, he said, "The world's passing you by. Don't you suspect anything?"

I said that I didn't know about him, but I didn't figure *anything* was passing *me* by. Any more than it was passing by anybody else, that is.

"No," he said. "No, you don't understand what I'm talking about."

He didn't elaborate on this point, and I didn't ask, because, to be perfectly frank, this is the kind of bullshit I don't much care about to begin with, and Winslow was close to wearing out his welcome. If I hadn't been pleased by his reason for being here, I would have bounced his ass out long ago.

Now he was sitting over there looking like he was half sick with guilt or anxiety or piles or something.

My wife once told me that I had a gift for the totally irrelevant, and I've always kind of cherished that remark.

Anyway, just then I saw Bucky ambling by the door, so I jumped over, swung it open and yelled, "Barfing dogs don't bite, Bucky!"

Bucky jumped about a foot to the side. Then he gave me a long, resentful look, and said, "Jesus, Rex, you're going to give a man a heart attack someday when you do that."

Winslow didn't say anything when I returned.

Local Man's Playful Ploy with Pun Perishes.

I started doing a small sign for my desk—the kind I keep hoping Cripps and Bucky will someday see and understand. I had an idea: I would use the "Rex says" approach, which until now I had used only on the big sign outside.

I started lettering it, then, and it went: "Why not grow up and be a horse? Don't be the same dumb ass you were yesterday!!!" I had never said specifically that these signs on my desk were meant for Cripps and Bucky, and I didn't really think they'd be offended by this one. If they understood it at all.

"You could make this place pretty decent, with a little imagination," Homer Winslow murmured suddenly, waving his pipe generally at the office. "Why don't you?"

"*Now* what's stuck up your ass?" I asked him. I dropped my ball point on the floor and leaned over, grunting, to pick it up.

"What you need is more than those horns, as impressive as they are," he said.

"They're antlers."

"Horns, antlers—they're all the same to me. What you need is pictures. I'm saying you need something to brighten up the place. A touch of art. See what I mean?"

I told him I did, but I was thinking I'd rather have naked walls than paintings like the dumb son of a bitch had hung on the walls of *his* office.

Just then I made a mistake on a letter.

"I'll be taking off the rest of the day," I told him, slamming the unfinished sign in the drawer.

I went outside, and Bucky came up to me and said, "How's the goddam spy doing?"

"Bucky," I said, "he isn't any spy. For Christ's sake, relax."

Bucky just kind of squinted his eyes and looked away from me. His hands were shoved halfway in his pockets and he shook them up and down, making his change and keys rattle.

"He's awful snoopy," Bucky said. "That's all I got to say."

"He's just got this silly-ass thing about being interested in people."

"Did he ask you the same thing?"

"You mean to tell him all about myself?"

Bucky nodded with his eyes closed.

"Well, yes, he did. But after all, he's a psychologist. That's his business, to study people."

"I don't care *what* he is," Bucky said, jerking at his pants. "I don't like nosy people. Some things just aren't any goddam business of people. And another thing: if he don't like it around this part of the country, why don't he just haul-ass *out?*"

"All right," I said. "Why don't you forget it? He isn't going to be here very much longer."

Before he turned away, Bucky mumbled, " 'Tell me all about yourself!' Shee-yut!"

Cripps was walking up as Bucky left, and I told them both I was getting out for a while.

Bucky said good-by, and Cripps waved. They didn't ask questions, because they knew my ways by now.

But as I was about to get in my car, I heard Cripps call out, "Who's the best?" and old Bucky came in right on cue, even though a little halfheartedly, with "Rex is best!"

This didn't cheer me up; not really. Still, it made me feel kind of good about my two boys. I'd sweeten their kitty before long, the way I did every now and then, by juggling the figures to make their sales look better. They didn't seem to be aware of my deception . . . or if they were, they didn't want to feel indebted to me. It's hard to accept favors, as everybody knows.

Of course, they probably didn't even notice. They are the type, I was thinking, that go through life missing goddam near everything.

I drove along to where County Route 163 crosses Alum Creek, down near Milford, and I spent the afternoon there by myself, drinking beer, slapping mosquitoes, pouring muddy water out of my shoes, and cussing civilization. I also stepped on the tip of my rod and broke the end-line guide. And my leg was bothering me. And I didn't catch any bass.

But all the time, right from the beginning, there was one other thing that was bothering me: what in the hell did I have to show for all my goddam years on earth? I don't get in these moods very often, but when I do, I'm really hit hard.

I don't mind saying I was in bad shape.

Prominent Local Auto Dealer Despondent.

13

Everything was all mixed up together, the way it always is. Sheila Richards, Cripp's bad stomach, Buckholz's fat idiocy, Winslow's irritating and mysterious presence. And worst of all, myself.

Like this Wingback Lake campaign. If ever a fourteen-carat stud outwitted himself, it was me. First of all, I manipulated myself right out of a peaceful place to fish. Granted, I knew this would happen, and I made enough money to take me and a couple others to Florida for a month of good living . . . still, have you seen Florida lately? There are too many characters cluttering up the landscape, with their pockets bulging from the profits of used-car campaigns.

The most depressing thing in the world, I keep thinking, is that there are just too goddam many people in it. I mean, I go out, like to this place on Alum Creek, and I am surrounded by trees and water. Fine. But then I think, Just over that hill I see in the distance is a gas-compressor station, and beyond that, a new electronics plant. Or, God help me, in the other direction, Rigolo's junkyard, which I have helped to fill.

When I think of this and then hear a blue jay start scratching the air with his call, I am depressed. Human beings, I say to myself, were not meant to live this way.

A man has got to have something to believe in.

Another day passed.

Then, on the next day, Clendon Metzger dropped by at the lot to tell me he was feeling all right. We talked for a while, and once he got so interested in what he was saying about his hemorrhoid operation, I was afraid the old son of a bitch was going to drop his pants and demonstrate.

He said that the doctor had discovered a hernia, too, and he would probably have to go back in the hospital sometime soon and have it corrected. He told me all this in the same loud cheerful voice that he always talks in, interspersed with enthusiastic comments on that goddam '66 Buick I had sold him.

But a funny thing—that I had kind of noticed before

but never paid much attention to—whenever I said something, old Metzger's mouth just eased open and his eyes kind of glazed over. If there was ever anybody sensitive to my charisma—the way some people are to poison ivy or goldenrod—it was Clendon Metzger.

I wondered if the professor was grinding away with his camera and sound track when I was talking to Metzger. But when I glanced at him, over Metzger's shoulder, I discovered something: he was not taking pictures and getting sound tapes of my *customers'* reactions to what I said, the way he'd told me. Absolutely not. I could tell by the angle of that suitcase, and by Winslow's reaction when I glanced up, that he was taking pictures of *me. I* was the star of this secret show he was filming.

Maybe Bucky was right, for once in his life, and old Winslow was some kind of spy.

Winslow left early that day, leaving his suitcase there in my office for a change. I took a long look at the thing a few times, but I didn't tamper with it. I wasn't bothered by what I had found out. Just kind of interested. I couldn't figure out any reason he had to blackmail me; but why, if he wanted to take my picture, didn't he just come out and ask me?

Bucky sold a Karmann Ghia to a retired plasterer named Jaro Christopher Mogez, believe it or not; and Cripps closed a deal over a '67 Chrysler, which we came close to taking a loss on, but Cripps needs a sale now and then, the way a depressed woman needs a new hairdo or dress. So I let him trade at a near loss for us, and then I juggled the trade-in allowance, so that Cripps made a few extra bucks.

I picked up the *Outdoor Life* and started reading an article on catching sturgeons in Arkansas. These fish go back to prehistoric times, and I have always been kind of fascinated that they have stuck around, like sharks and crustaceans and other vestiges. Life must have been dangerous then, but I'll bet it was exciting and beautiful.

I can never read over five or ten minutes straight without looking up and sighing and fidgeting and scratching my ass and dropping something and lighting a Dutch Masters cigar or something. This gives my wife the pip, because she thinks she is some kind of intellectual. The culmination of Western culture, practically, and I am a gross but energetic garage mechanic she lets live with her providing I keep my hands washed with Lava soap and don't irritate her too much. She was made homecoming queen one year in college, and I view her moral downfall as beginning about that time.

Anyway I have this short attention span, so one of the times I look up from the article on catching sturgeons, I see a well-built woman standing kind of lost and forlorn near a VW, and damned if it isn't Sheila Richards herself. Cripps is just walking up towards her (Bucky is out with a customer in a '69 Mustang), and I see them both kind of stop. She says something, and Cripps turns and says something as he faces the office, where I am sitting looking back at both of them, with my thumb in the *Outdoor Life* and my stomach feeling kind of funny.

Part of what I had decided before I met Sheila again was to be wise and a little dignified and behave myself. And act my age. Not only that, I wasn't sure how much truth there might be in that sentence in Taylor Hall. Since our town is small, and the college, too, there was a goddam good chance there were not two Sheila Richardses to share the fame of that report. After all, she might be known as the town pump in circles beyond my immediate influence. Also, she might be carrying a dose of clap.

But, of course, seeing her out there made everything go

down the drain, and I stood up and straightened out my string tie and moved out towards her. She was wearing those shorts that look like a miniskirt, and her dimpled knees looked very cute, I thought. She was also wearing eye shadow, or mascara, or something. Whatever she was wearing, it was obvious that Sheila Richards did not view herself as a conservative woman. She might have been a back-to-nature girl, but she believed in going back to nature looking as seductive as possible.

"Well, look who's here," I said, walking up to her. "Local Beauty Visits Czar of Cars."

"Hello," she said. She didn't look in my eyes, but straight at my string tie.

"I thought maybe you'd gone over to my competition," I said. "Or left for parts unknown."

"No," she said, sinking a brief glance in my eyes. "I've been around." Then she looked over my shoulder and said, "I've had the most awful case of poison ivy you've ever heard of. I haven't been able to do anything at all except go to work and go home."

"That's too bad," I said. "I wonder where you got it?"

She flicked a disgusted look past my eyes and said, "Oh, you!"

"Have you thought some more about the VW?" I asked her.

She just kind of looked numb at that, and started biting her lip. I could tell she wasn't looking at the car at all.

I decided to help her out. "How about hearing a little poetry?" I said.

She frowned at me and said, "What?" She looked wary.

Then I recited an old favorite of mine:

> "The other day I heard of a man
> Who died from drinking beer out of an
> old tomato can.

Now drinking beer can't kill a man,
But an old . . . tomato . . . can."

When I finished, she put the tips of the fingers of both her hands to her temples and said, "What?"

"Emily Dickinson," I said.

"What is?"

"That poem. That's who wrote it."

She kind of laughed then, and said, "Honestly, I could listen to you talk for hours on end, but I can't understand half of what you're *saying!* I suppose that sounds silly, doesn't it?"

"Come on," I said, rubbing her arm a little. "We'll take it out again and see how it handles."

Her eyes snapped into place, and she stared right at me. "The VW?"

I nodded. "That, too," I said.

"You're awful!" she said.

"Come on. Let's go."

"Where to?"

"Anywhere you want to take it," I said. "Phoenix, Minneapolis, Port Said, Jamaica . . ." This is one of my standard jokes, but Sheila Richards just nodded soberly and chewed on her lip some more, as if she were really trying to decide which one of those places to choose.

"I *would* like to talk to you," she said.

"Fine," I said. "Wait'll I slap some dealer plates on, and we'll give it a whirl."

I put the plates on, wondering if I was sounding too goddam professional, and when I stood up, Sheila Richards was standing there with her hands folded in front of her, and—so help me—looking kind of lost. There was a sign I'd printed and put on the windshield that said, "The only thing used about this baby is the title." I took the sign off and put it on the car next to it, which happened to be an old, busted-up '64 Renault with rotten gears and tires like soiled Kleenex.

Then I helped Sheila into the driver's seat of the VW, but no breast brush this time, although I did jam her thigh accidentally with my knee. I apologized, and she just looked at me and gave me a kind of exasperated sigh. It was like she'd known my ways for years.

For some reason, I was feeling kind of sorry for her. She didn't even act like the same girl who had zapped me that day, and had later tossed her happy silver panties out on the grass.

I lighted a Dutch Masters panetela when she angled the car out of the lot, and said, "Hope you don't mind these things. I know a lot of women think they stink."

"No," she said, "I don't mind."

I patted her knee and then the inside of her bare thigh, and said, "Come on, what's the matter with you? You act unhappy."

"Don't do that, please," she said. "You'll make me wreck the car."

She took the VW out on the highway, and then turned in the opposite direction from Wingback Lake. I figured that might have been symbolic, but I have to confess I was interested in hearing what she wanted to talk about, even if she kept her silver panties on. I kind of wanted to talk with her, too, but I wasn't sure what about. I had thought I would ask her if she knew anybody at the college, maybe somebody who worked in Taylor Hall or something. That sounded pretty direct, but of course she wouldn't know anything about her name being above the fourth urinal.

We drove along the highway a while, and then she turned off on a country road.

"I certainly do hope you don't think all of this is just a waste of time," she said.

"Thousands Suffer from Baldness," I said.

She reached over and slapped my arm, saying, "Now stop saying those silly, crazy things. Can't you see I'm trying to be serious?"

"All right," I said.

"Well, I just don't want you to think all of this is just a waste of time."

Right then I realized she had been making noises like this all along—asking me if I minded her driving this far, and how long I could be away from the lot, etc. She seemed so nervous, I began to figure maybe it was her time of the month or something. That was exactly the way she acted. I wouldn't have been too surprised if she'd pulled the car over to the side of the road and started bawling.

But she didn't. For about the fifth time, she said, "I want to talk to you, and you don't help things a bit!"

"What do you mean?" I asked her.

"Do you realize," she said, with her voice getting shrill, "that I don't even know what to *call* you?"

"Why, call me Rex," I said. "What else?"

"Well, all I knew was your last name. And for heaven's sake, I didn't want to go around calling you Mr. McCoy after what happened the other day."

"Yes," I said. "I see what you mean. I thought everybody knew my name was Rex. It's in all the ads."

"I don't read that part of the newspaper," she said.

"Actually, it's Regius," I said, "but everybody calls me either Rex or Mac."

"Well, maybe everybody does, but I didn't."

I contemplated that sentence for a while, and then Sheila suddenly turned the VW down a little side road that dwindled out into some woods beside a stream. It was right beside a part of Alum Creek that I had never fished, although I had wondered about it now and then when I was driving by.

Sheila turned the ignition off and shifted around in her seat to look at me.

"I've thought a lot about the other day out there at the lake," she said. "Or the other evening, I mean. With that awful old woman coming by and everything. And do you know something, I just feel terrible."

"About what?" I asked her.

"You must certainly think I'm awfully cheap," she said in a warbly voice.

"I do not. Not at all. Absolutely not."

Sheila took a cigarette and tapped it against the steering wheel, and I lighted it for her.

"I certainly do hope nothing like that happens again," she said. "I almost died when that old witch came up with the flashlight."

"So did I," I said. "Elderly Woman Foils Sex Crime."

"Do you realize how *cheap* and . . . and how *sordid* everything must have looked?"

"I suppose so."

"Never again," Sheila said, exhaling smoke. "And then there's *you*. God knows what *you* must think of me!"

"I can settle your mind about that," I said, tapping the ash off my cigar out the window. "I think you're a very desirable and attractive and . . . *sweet* young girl."

"Bullshit!"

"What?"

"You heard me. Bullshit! Look, if there's anything I don't want, it's lies. I've had enough of them for a lifetime. You have no idea!"

"Well, what I meant was . . ."

"What's *sweet* about me? Now I ask you, what's *sweet* about a girl who you can make love to on a blanket right down on the ground the second time you have her out, and she doesn't even know your first name? I ask you."

"Names don't mean much," I said. "I mean, not always."

"No, they don't," she said, "but sometimes they do."

I reached over and pulled her against me, and kissed her cheek and neck here and there, until she turned her mouth towards me. When I kissed her on the mouth, she opened her sweet little birdy lips and kind of hummed with pleasure.

Finally, she pulled back and said in a tidy voice, "Not here, Rex."

"I know a motel about eleven miles from here," I said. Actually it was sixteen. Prominent Auto Dealer Lies Again. "Let's go there."

She blinked her eyes rapidly several times, which I naturally understood to mean yes, so I walked around the VW and got in the driver's seat. She was patting her hair in place as she looked in the mirror fastened to the back of the sunshade.

"I certainly do hope you don't think I'm cheap," she said. "You don't, do you?"

"Absolutely not," I told her. "After all, when two adults . . ."

Right at this time, I was pulling out onto the highway, and a big semi outfit hauling pipe came by, passing a constipated '68 MG. So I concentrated on navigating out into the center lane, without even bothering to finish the sentence. Sheila Richards didn't seem to notice.

The motel was called the Lakeview Terrace Motel, which sounds like the name of about every other motel I have ever stayed in.

I didn't know anyone there, so I figured it was as safe as something like this is likely to be. Anyway, a fat old woman wearing a hearing aid signed us in, under the name of Mr. and Mrs. Harry Biddle, Cleveland, Ohio.

Harry Biddle and I were in the Marines together, and

we once—it must have been early in 1943—made a vow that if and when we got back to the States, we would always sign hotel registers with each other's name . . . providing we were doing some extracurricular screwing, which at the time was the only kind we were thinking of.

Harry Biddle was killed by a mine explosion on Iwo the day after I was blown up almost identically (I heard about it later in the hospital), and for a while after the war I would sometimes say to myself, "Rex, you got two lives to live now. Because there was nobody around who knew the Harry Biddle you did, and if you don't live his life—or at least some part of it—who will?"

Ex-Marine Vows Vengeance on Death.

Anyway, I signed us in and then went out to the VW, where Sheila was nervously smoking a cigarette and looking out at the world through big, dark, sexy sunglasses. Behind the glasses, she looked like a scared little bug, so I asked her if she wanted a drink at the bar, but she said no thanks, so we went into the room and Sheila turned on the television.

There was an afternoon quiz show on, and I turned it off. She turned it right back on, but I turned it off again. Then I kissed her and started undressing both of us, and when I came to her brassière, she just sat there with her hands folded in her lap and her eyes closed. I couldn't figure her out. I guess it was just the mood she was in. Anyway, she finally had to help me with the clasps in back, because, like every goddam brassière I have ever seen, it wasn't made to be worked with male hands. Or at least my hands. This is one place where a woman has to help herself, if she is going to be respectably raped.

When we were both naked, we lay back on the bed and I caressed her and hugged her and kissed her for about two weeks, until we finally got down to business. All the time her eyes were closed. And I am happy to report that there was nothing wrong with her springs, no matter *how* much mileage she had.

When we finished, we lay there side by side, breathing long and deep, and when Sheila asked me what name I had used, I told her the story of Harry Biddle.

She was quiet a few minutes, and then she said, "Rex, do you know something?"

"What?" I said.

"You are a very sensitive person underneath that rough exterior."

I wasn't sure whether that was a compliment or an insult, but I was too peaceful and satisfied with everything to care.

Then she examined her thigh with her index finger and said, "I'm going to have a bruise there, where you jabbed me with your knee."

"It's symbolic," I said, and she slapped my arm playfully.

A few minutes later, the bed squeaked and Sheila got up to light a cigarette. She went to the drapes, pulled them aside and peeked through.

"There's a swimming pool out there," she said.

"There almost always is," I told her.

She watched some kids swim for a while, and then she came back and snuggled up beside me.

I was almost asleep when she surprised me by asking, "Rex, do you *really* think I'm sweet?"

I said I was sure of it, which seemed to please her.

Once or twice, she mentioned that she certainly hoped I didn't think she was cheap or an easy lay. Naturally, I told her I didn't.

She was drowsy and comfortable there beside me for a long time, and then she started talking about her past—a divorced husband (or a husband she was separated from

. . . she was vague about this), and a three-year-old daughter with her parents out West. And her previous job, which was as a secretary for the history department on campus. That was before she started working for T. F. Hanaway.

Eventually, she went to sleep. I lay there, too, and dozed off once or twice myself during the next hour.

As we were driving back to town, I asked her what the last words she wanted to hear were.

"I don't know," she said.

" 'Hello, deh. Ah is yoh new NEIGH-buh!' "

For a second she was absolutely quiet, and I was afraid the joke hadn't gone over any better with her than it had with old man Metzger. But then she laughed real loud and fast, rapidly dusting some of my cigar ashes off her lap. I figured she was just laughing to please me. There was something phony about that laugh. A couple seconds later, I adjusted the rear-vision mirror and glanced at her eyes, and they were a thousand miles away.

I figured maybe she was a liberal and didn't think racial jokes like that were in good taste. And I was about ready to tell her that I didn't really have anything against Negroes. I was going to mention all the favors I had done for Willie Byrd; but I realized that wouldn't work, so I didn't say anything.

If she had been offended by the joke, nothing I could say now would help. And any explanation would probably sound phony.

I just kept my mouth shut until we got back into town.

She seemed happy enough when I let her out of the car, however, so everything was just fine.

Abducted Woman Returns Safely.

14

The next morning I woke up and just stayed in bed for a while, thinking. I didn't want to go down to the lot, where I would have to face Bucky and Cripps and Professor Winslow, who was secretly taking pictures of me and recording my voice and Christ knows what all, for Christ knows what reason. And maybe Rick Ruggles and Willie Byrd.

I just lay there for a while, and then the mailman drove by in his little red, white, and blue truck, so I went outside and got a couple of bills, a letter from our boy, and a postcard from my wife, which was written entirely in Spanish.

I read our boy's letter first. He's in college, weighs about 230, and he's got long hair and a beard. He's always been a very tense kid. Naturally, the letter was really written to my wife, although it was addressed to both of us.

Since my wife wasn't home, I figured I would open the envelope and read the boy's latest complaint against a world he thinks his mother and I personally, and with malice aforethought, created for his personal bewilderment, distaste, and frustration.

The letter was typewritten on cheap yellow paper, and the ribbon was so bad that the type was the color of cobwebs, so I practically went blind trying to read the goddam thing. But here's the way it went:

Dear Folks,

Maybe you've heard about the disturbances on our campus since I wrote to you last, and you have probably wondered if I am involved in them. I am afraid the answer is yes. I won't go into details as to my feelings, as well as the reasoning behind my convictions, because in all honesty I do not think you and Dad would understand. I know that must sound terribly snobbish and everything, and naturally it doesn't have anything to do with natural intelligence or knowledge of the world. Rather, I think it has to do with the fact that your intelligence was expended in getting information about a world that is not only different from, but ultimately irrelevant to, the world we who are young today must face.

Why do I bother telling you all this, when it can't help but cause pain? Because I believe you have a right to know, even if the reasons for my actions are inaccessible.

This is probably all very incoherent, and it probably sounds very egotistical to you, but one of my professors recently said that it is "an honest man's duty to make himself misunderstood by others; otherwise, he simply is not honest." I believe that.

I don't think you can accuse me of bugging you for money all the time, but I do find that I need some now, to take care of laundry (Dad won't believe this, but I do keep myself clean, in spite of my beard and long hair), and to pay for books, supplies, some new clothes, etc. If you could spare two hundred, I could make it last the quarter.

Mother, when do you leave for Spain? It sounds like a fine trip. Enjoy yourself, and give Denise my best. Also Dad, and tell him I don't need a car. My Honda's just great, and all I need. But tell him thanks, anyway. No one can ever say he isn't generous with money.

As Ever,
Phil

I sat down and wrote a $205 check for him, and a note telling him to spend the extra five dollars for a new typewriter ribbon, and a haircut.

When I finished with this, I picked up the postcard from my wife and just stared at the Spanish for a couple minutes, wondering why she would do a crazy thing like this to me.

Now I took Spanish when I was in high school, because I heard it was the easiest language there was. I managed to flunk it, anyway, the second semester. Our teacher was a fat little bachelor with teary eyes that he was always rubbing with his pudgy little fist, and he wore high-topped shoes. Every now and then I wonder what ever happened to him.

Anyway, my wife keeps telling me I already practically know the language, and would be able to learn it perfectly if I only relaxed and spoke it around the house with her. What she can't seem to get through her expensively coiffured head is that I don't *want* to learn the goddam language. If, by some kind of dirty trick, I woke up one morning and found out I *had* learned the goddam language, I would try to figure out some way to *forget* the goddam language.

Local Businessman Says Speak American.

This is what I can't get through my wife's head. When I try to tell her this, she says I am being defensive, or defeatist, and that all my bluster is just a cover-up for feelings of intellectual and cultural inferiority.

If there is anybody in this world my charisma has never worked on, it is my wife.

So now I am faced with this postcard with every word in Spanish. I don't know if she is dying, or in bed with another man, or taking up LSD or bullfighting, or what. All I see is the way she signs the letter: *"Hasta la vista."* Reading this, I remember all the times I have kissed her good-by in the morning, and she has said, *"Hasta la vista,"* as if that will trigger some deep impulse in me, and I will come back and talk to her like Cesar Romero or some goddam Spanish body.

There is also the morning newspaper out there, in a little box beside the mailbox, so I shake it out and give it the onceover, but there's not much that's interesting. Mostly just the same old trouble.

Then I get dressed, shove the postcard in my pocket so that I can go over it later and maybe figure out where she is staying, and go down to Gestler's Lunch, where I order breakfast in spite of what their sign says. I keep telling them they should change it to Gestler's Café, instead of Lunch.

"People should use words accurately," I tell them, "or how can you communicate? If you mean lunch, say lunch; but if you mean lunch, breakfast, dinner, and snacks, then say something else."

Gestler just listens and nods, but he doesn't know what I'm talking about, and the name stays the same.

I always like a big breakfast, and this morning I ordered two eggs over light on top of corned-beef hash, with toast and jelly, V-8 juice and black coffee, which for some reason I had ordered every morning since my wife left. Sally, the waitress, should know by now what I will order, but she always asks me anyway, like she has never seen me before. She isn't the brightest girl in the world, or even the second brightest.

When I am drinking my second cup of coffee and about to light up my first Dutch Masters of the day, I stare for a while at the building opposite, where T. F. Hanaway's office is located, and then I notice, in the window I am looking through, a cheap sign announcing hillbilly music by a group called the Hatfield Four. The sign says they are going to be playing at the Lewistown Grange Hall on May 15 through May 22, both of which dates are already long past. Lewistown is a little bitty place about thirty miles away. At the top of the poster is a picture of these four fellows wearing cowboy hats and boots.

It was funny, because the name should have been enough, but I really didn't get the idea then. The idea didn't come until later. All I did was kid Sally about having that sign still in the window, because it was already June. There was no telling where the Hatfield quartet was by now. Maybe in heaven, or jail.

All Sally said was, "Frank put it up and forgot to take it down." Frank is Frank Gestler, the owner.

A dirty little kid came in—about eight or nine—and ordered a milkshake. I signaled to Sally that I'd pay for it. The kid looked like he might be one of Cripps's nephews, which he has about forty thousand of in this county alone. That kid will buy a car from me someday, when he grows up. Make no mistake.

I finally got around to lighting the Dutch Masters, and walked out, where who should I run into but T. F. Hanaway himself, talking to Bill Knowles, the U.S. agricultural agent for the county. I slapped them on the shoulder when I walked by and thought a little about Sheila Richards until I got to my car. I was wondering if maybe she was carrying a dose. It would be a hell of a note if a man in my position in town, who was last year's sergeant at arms for Rotary, came down with the clap, or worse, for God's sake; although it wouldn't be the first time. I mean for a prominent figure to get a dose.

I kept thinking about the sign above the fourth urinal in Taylor Hall. One thing sure: it wasn't any goddam lie. On the way back to the lot, there was a fire call, and I had to wait third in line behind a red light for eight minutes until it was all clear. All the time, I was thinking about

Professor Homer Winslow, and wondering what in the hell he was up to. I decided to try to get him to open up, and maybe he would spill everything.

When I got there, he hadn't arrived yet. Cripps was sitting at my desk, smoking a Marlboro and signing his name to some lists of specials I'd had mimeographed a few days earlier. Bucky was sitting on the edge of the desk, talking about the Redlegs' pitching. He's got this idea in his head that he's an authority on pitching. One of his great subjects is, "Does a curve ball really curve?" And his stand is affirmative. Loud, passionate, angry, martyred, spitting, fist-pounding affirmative.

Sometimes I think Bucky is bad for Cripps's stomach. Along with Cripps smoking too many cigarettes. And at such times, I wonder where two such card-carrying freaks as these two sons of bitches could ever work, except here. And then I feel sorry for thinking it. Because these boys really aren't so bad.

Cripps suddenly quit right in the middle of the specials he was signing, and said he was going to check out a 1970 Mustang we had just taken in. I happened to watch him for a couple of minutes after he left, since I didn't have anything better to do. He got in the driver's seat, switched on the lights, then got out and looked them over. He got back in the driver's seat and just sat there for a few seconds. I could tell he didn't have any idea he was being watched.

He picked his nose a little bit, sighed, kind of gazed around, and then pulled out a Marlboro and punched in the cigarette lighter. After he lit it, he just sat there and smoked a while.

The phone rang, and I answered it. It was a man named Jennings, and he started complaining about a Mercury, '68 or '69 (I can't remember which), that Bucky had sold him a month before. He went on and on for a while, but I only half listened. It was something about the transmission noise, and he thought he was going to have trouble with it, which I didn't doubt but didn't give a damn about, since he couldn't touch us—the dumb bastard should have had more brains than to buy it in the first place.

I made ambiguous noises whenever it was expected of me, and kind of let Jennings unwind. I have this theory that if you listen too hard to someone else bitching, you're doing him a disservice, because you're encouraging him in his self-pity. Bitching is sick.

Anyway, my bad leg itched and hurt a little, and I kept saying such things as "That's too bad" and "Son of a bitch!" until Jennings unwound and hung up. Then I got to my feet, stretched my leg and walked over to the door . . . and there was old Cripps, exactly as I had left him, sitting in the Mustang.

He had put his cigarette out, and was just sitting there, like somebody had hit him over the head with a hammer and he hadn't started to fall over yet, which is exactly the way most people spend their lives. I can't stand it the way these boys of mine waste time. They don't have the first idea about how to make a dollar.

So I went over to Cripps, and gave him Bucky's favorite opener: "Cripps, how's it going? Something wrong?"

Old Cripps angled one eye up at me, and the other shot over towards Indianapolis somewhere, and he said, "Oh, hell, Rex. Nothing."

Which of course meant "something," the way he said it. So I said, "Come on. Out with it, and maybe I can help."

"Rex," he said, reaching for another one of the loose Marlboros in his shirt pocket, "I'm worried."

"Is that so?" I said. I got out a Dutch Masters panetela, and we both lit up.

"Damn right," Cripps said, exhaling over the steering wheel.

When he didn't go on, I thought I'd get him started on

something else and kind of circle around to what was eating him. "This baby check out okay?" I said, slapping the Mustang on the roof.

Cripps looked up at me kind of surprised, and then said, "Oh, yeah. So far, it's okay. Lights work."

Jesus Christ! He'd been out here twenty minutes, and all he'd checked was the goddam lights, windshield wipers, and cigarette lighter.

"Try the horn," I said, trying to keep my temper.

"Oh, it's okay," Cripps said. Then he pushed it with his thumb, but it just made a soggy little sound.

"Doesn't sound real good," I said. It was quite an understatement.

"I thought it was all right," Cripps said, trying to sound surprised.

"Cripps," I said, "what's eating you?"

"You're shrewd," he said then. "I guess you can tell I'm in trouble."

"It's obvious," I said. "You don't have to be a genius to figure that out."

"Well, Rex," he said, "it's money. My debts are getting me down. I tell you, I'm worried."

"Everybody's over his head in debt," I said. "It's the country's greatest pastime. Hell, it's nothing to worry about."

"I'm not lighthearted about such things the way you are," he said, as if he resented my good spirits. "Things get me down. I don't mind saying they worry me."

"Well, hell, get busy and *make* more money," I said. "Nobody's stopping you!"

Cripps cast an agonized look at me and said, "Hell, that's easy to say, but goddammit, Rex, not everybody's got your knack for selling."

"Get in there and fight, boy! Get in there and give 'em

hell. Go out nights, get on the phone, call up your friends, go over your old sales records of two years ago, and talk those people into getting another car from old Cripps. Don't take no for an answer. Think positive, think big, *think!* Hell, I'll give you some of my two- and three-year-old leads, if you want! Sure. Right now. Come on up to the office!"

Cripps just kind of strained, like he was constipated. Then he repeated something that almost made me want to knock his goddam head off. "Rex," he said, "that's easier said than done."

"Oh, shit," I groaned. "Oh, Technicolor, wrapped-in-gauze, plastic-protected, Sanforized, homogenized, chlorophyl-treated *shit*!"

"What's the matter?" Cripps asked, looking a little alarmed.

So I tried to calm down and talk reasonably to him. After all, what was the use? So I said something about just relaxing and "waiting for the breaks," and other excuses that would get through to that jelly-bean brain of his. And so help me, he drank it all up the way a thirsty man drinks water.

"So what's the use of worrying?" I said, finally. "Just remember one of my favorite sayings, and repeat it whenever you begin to feel low: 'I don't care if the apples don't grow; I'll live on applesauce.' "

I've always thought that was kind of witty and wise, but it was lost on Cripps. He stared straight ahead a second, and then he got a shrewd look, and said, "Yeah, Rex, but if the apples don't grow, how are you going to get applesauce?"

I stared back at him, then, trying to see if he was putting me on. I couldn't believe it, but I swear it was the truth. The poor dumb son of a bitch was serious.

So after a few seconds, I said, "Yeah, I guess you got a

point there." And then I walked away, so goddam disgusted I could have fired the nincompoop right then and there.

When I got near the office, I threw my Dutch Masters away half smoked. I've been doing that a lot lately. The asphalt all around the door to our office is covered with three- and four-inch stubs, like bleached and dried-up little doggie turds.

Right then, I saw Winslow park his suitcase—which he had taken with him this time—between the VWs we've got lined up on one side of the front row for the college trade.

The dent in his forehead was a little deeper, and I figure he had a headache. When he comes in, I tell him we have some aspirin in the drawer, but he pinches the bridge of his nose, like Louis Calhern playing Julius Caesar, and says, "Aspirin I don't need."

Bucky gets off the desk and jerks at his crotch. Maybe one of these days he will buy a pair of pants that fit him, and don't twist his balls up into his lungs. I think he wears his pants too small to give him the illusion he isn't quite so fat.

"You notice?" Winslow asked.

"I notice what?" I asked back.

"I have a headache. How did you know?"

I didn't want to tell him about the dent in his forehead, because I figured it might hurt his feelings, so I just said, "Oh, something about the expression on your face."

"My wife can tell, too," he commented, nodding.

"I'm going out to get some coffee," Bucky said. "Anybody want some?" I noticed he still wouldn't look at our professor in residence.

Cripps said he didn't want any, but Winslow and I told Bucky to bring us one black, one with cream and sugar. I paid.

Cripps went out to take a '68 Rambler to a prospect, and when Bucky returned, he had a customer waiting for him—a guy from the fire department who has been thinking of a '70 Chevy.

So Winslow and I were alone there in the office. He had just lighted his pipe, and he was holding it upside down in one hand, and the coffee cup in the other.

He lifted the coffee and said, "To the day of our liberation from this place."

"How come you don't haul-ass out of this place, if it bugs you so much?" I asked him.

For a second, he stared at me angrily, as if I had just attacked his right to free speech. "It's too complicated," he said. "Not only that, you wouldn't understand. Let's just say you're happy in a place like this, and I'm not. Let's just keep it like that."

I looked about three inches inside his head, then, and said, "Why you hairy little shit, you don't know whether I'd understand or not. Not only that, some of those things you understand might not even be true."

"How could I understand them then?" Winslow cried.

"My point, precisely," I said.

For a few seconds, he brooded and pulled on the tips of his mustache. He'd laid his pipe on the edge of my desk, by a sign that read, "Opportunity knocks but 2,583,196 times."

"I might have known you'd get personal," he said finally, in a quiet voice.

"What about you?" I asked. "Listen, this is my town, where I have built up my business, and where I've got my own friends . . . and where we all get along pretty goddam well, without some arrogant son of a bitch coming in and trying to tell us how fucking backward we are, or illiterate or bigoted or whatever in Christ's sake your bitch is. So my advice is this: love it or leave it."

"I might have known you'd come up with something like that," Winslow said. "Shit!"

"Or," I said, "shape up or ship out."

"Very eloquent," he said. "Very eloquent!"

"Drink your coffee," I said. "Before it gets cold."

He nodded, as if he recognized the reasonableness of what I'd said; he picked up the cup and blew on the coffee.

We sat there sipping our coffee for a few minutes, and then Winslow said, "Actually, you got a point. I shouldn't have opened up like that. My nerves are tearing apart, for Christ's sake. Headaches, department politics, the whole goddam place . . . you know, I can't get used to the tempo of life around here. It may be all right for you and your salesmen, but after you've spent all your life in New York, well . . . hell, nothing less will do."

"Who said it *is* less?"

"Look," Winslow said, "I'm trying to make it right. Okay? That's just my way of speaking, for Christ's sake. Everybody around here is so fucking touchy, I don't know where to turn. Let me tell you something: after you've lived in the city, a place like this seems like a mausoleum. And it's affecting my wife and kids. My wife has hives, my kids aren't learning anything in school and their teachers hate them . . . I'm telling you, it's no fucking picnic. I don't know how long we can hold out. I'm not shitting you, it's that serious."

"Well, I figure if you keep busy, you're happy. No matter where you are."

"You think I don't keep busy? You think I'm lazy like the rest of these . . . these people around here? Listen, Rex . . . may I call you Rex?"

"Everybody else does, and as a matter of fact I told you to call me Rex when you first came here."

"All right. Listen, Rex, there are some things you can't help. Right? I mean, you grow up in New York, where the excitement and the pace are like a whole different world . . . anyway, you grow up there and adjust to it, and your whole value system of expectations is adjusted to that, and then suddenly, wham, you're out here in a town of fifteen thousand, filled with retired farmers who have never seen a stage play or gone to a symphony or voted anything but Republican in their whole life. Let me tell you: it's not easy. It's not easy."

"All right, why don't you leave, then?"

But Winslow didn't hear me. He held his cup of coffee next to his chest and shook his head back and forth. "And then there's this project I'm engaged in. Nobody understands the necessity of what I'm doing, or even the validity."

"Incidentally, what *is* this study of yours, anyway?"

The question stopped his head from shaking back and forth, and his eyes fixed on something vague in the distance. Then they shifted around and looked at me.

"Rex," he said, after a few seconds, "why are you asking?"

"I just wanted to know."

"Let me make it easy for you," he said. "Let's not play games any more. You know. Right?"

"Local Dealer Suspects Fraud," I said.

"How long?"

"Oh, a few days."

"I figured you knew."

"How did you figure that out?"

"You forget," he said, closing his eyes and sloshing his coffee, "I really *am* a specialist in nonverbal communication, like I've been telling you. I've picked up the little glances you send toward my suitcase. I could measure the difference in your stance, the position of your shoulders, even, after a certain period. That would be the exact time you caught on. I figure it was about last Monday. Yes, I figured you'd catch on."

Then I asked him what in the hell he *was* doing, taking *my* picture instead of pictures of my customers, and why he hadn't leveled with me from the start.

"Listen," he said, shaking his head back and forth as he looked at me, "I'm saying you already know the reason."

"Which is?"

"I have already told you."

"You mean my charisma."

Winslow nodded. "I mean your charisma."

"I thought that had to do with swaying crowds or something. You know, the great orator or actor or something."

"It's usually thought of that way," he said. "But like I've told you before: I'm saying that this is also an interpersonal phenomenon. Essentially the same thing, you know what I mean?"

"You mean, this is why I am a good salesman. Is that it?"

"You have absolutely no idea how much of this thing you have got. It's like voltage—the voltage of personality, the irradiation of conviction, of power, charm, magic, whatever you want to call it. You have no idea. I'm talking about the raw power of personal magnetism. Voice inflection, voice timbre, eye focus, stance, gestures, facial expression . . . all of these things are part of the communicative act. This thing doesn't necessarily make friends; it can just as easily keep people away. Maybe a little bit afraid. Awed. I've never seen all of these qualities in just the right mix until I saw you go to work."

"I don't know how to figure this out," I said. "How did you find out about me in the first place?"

"I came in here to buy a Galaxie," he said. "You didn't have a '66, which is the one I wanted, but I remember talking with you a couple of minutes. I was full of this fucking study of mine, but it was funny: I didn't really catch on to this gift of yours until I'd left and was looking at a Galaxie over at Stimson's Lot, on River Street. I realized you'd almost sold me a '68 Impala, and that wasn't what I'd made up my mind to buy, and you hadn't even had a chance to get wound up."

"Old Stimson's got some decent stock now and then," I said.

"Well, that's where I got my car, anyway. When I was over there, I snapped my fingers and said to myself, Wait a minute. That man was it! He was a living, breathing demonstration of what I am studying."

"So you decided to get out your camera and tapes and measure me, to see what made me tick."

"You got the idea."

I didn't say anything for a couple seconds. Winslow had put his coffee cup down and was relighting his pipe.

"I've got a couple of thousand feet of you on film," he said. "When I get it all edited, we'll have a closely measured, detailed study of your particular brand of supereffective bullshit at work. It'll be something new, believe me."

"You didn't want me to know about it because it would make me self-conscious. Is that it?"

"You've hit it," he said.

"Well," I said, "I'm not exactly the self-conscious type. In fact, my wife says I have the sensitivity of a water buffalo. Not that she's ever seen one."

"What do you hear from your wife?"

On an impulse, I pulled out the postcard and gave it to him. "I just got this card in the mail this morning. You know Spanish?"

"A little bit. Let me see."

But he couldn't make it out either, beyond *"mañana," "Hasta la vista,"* and a couple other words.

"I wonder why she wrote it in Spanish," Winslow said, "when you don't read the language."

I told him it made her feel superior, and she also had a gift for being wrongheaded.

"Well," he said after a bit. "I guess I've got all the film I need."

"I never realized I would be a movie star," I said.

"You know," Winslow said, jabbing his pipe at me, "I'm going to keep in touch. Maybe come back and take some more film. I can't impress on you how rare this thing is. The mere fact it hasn't ever been measured before or given a precise name doesn't mean there isn't this reality in our lives. What I'm trying to do, in a sense, is give us a vocabulary for this, and make the words something precise and identifiable, after I work it all out."

"It's still kind of hard to believe," I said. "You mention gestures, for instance. Hell, man, I'm about the third- or fourth-clumsiest man alive!"

"Clumsy, you're not," Winslow said. "You've got the gestures of a ballet dancer, believe it or not. At least you do when you're going through your pitch. Other times, maybe you're clumsy. Possibly you *want* to be clumsy, subconsciously. You know, *afflict* other people for some reason. Express deep, unconscious aggressions. But when the chips are down . . .

"Listen, I'm trying to measure the shape of how we relate to others. Second, since this is obviously connected with what *most* people mean by charisma, why it's the thing that sways crowds, multitudes, nations. I'm saying it's the raw power that relates all of us to others, or sends nations into war, or causes them to seek peace. Can you name anything *more* important, offhand?"

"Maybe I should have gone into politics," I said.

Then Winslow shot a look three inches deep. "Listen," he said, "what we couldn't do if we got you onto a platform someplace, speaking out for the right ideas. We could begin right here. I'm talking about the school levy for next year, and about race prejudice all around us. Listen, if you believe in these ideas, there's no telling what we could do!"

I had just been kidding about politics, but old Winslow there was looking serious. His mustache and hair were all bristled out with excitement.

"There's so much to be done!" he said. He shook his head several times, and I asked him what the trouble was.

He closed his eyes and said, "The trouble is that you appear to have soaked up all the provincial attitudes of this place, and you evidently don't feel the important, the critical issues that are all around us. I mean, if you just had more of a social conscience, instead of only caring about cars, and fishing, and hunting wild moose . . ."

"That's an elk," I said.

"Elk," he went on. "I mean, if you only had some understanding of the *crises* we're in these days . . . Jesus Christ, man!"

"Monkeys Take Over Zoo," I said.

"Look I don't mean to be hostile or put you down or anything, but living in a sleepy little college town like this, how could you *expect* to understand where we are? You've lived here all your life, haven't you?"

"Except for three years in the Gyrenes," I told him.

"Well, that's hardly the kind of exposure I had in mind," he said.

Then he seemed to think of something, and he got several folders and pamphlets out of his briefcase and said, "Here. Read this material. I just want to see how you react."

"To see if I pass some kind of test, is that it?"

Winslow closed his eyes and shook his head no. "There you go again. Don't be defensive. I just want to hear your reaction. Okay? This project's eating up my life, but I've got to find out a few things. That's not much to ask. Okay?"

I looked at the pamphlets. One was titled *The Chronic Crisis of the Cities: A Problem in Black and White*; and another one was *The Revolution in Wealth.*

"Sure," I told him. "I'll look them over."

Bucky came back then and asked me to go over a '67 Corvette as a trade-in on a '69 T-Bird. I glanced in my yellow book, then shoved the book in my pocket and walked into the action.

The car belonged to a grocer from Milford who had two fingers off his left hand. When I got through with it, Bucky and I walked away, and I whispered to him how high we could go but that he ought to try to skin it a hundred for the sake of our overhead.

Bucky nodded with his eyes shut, like he had just heard some confidential information about the Cincinnati pitching staff. He has a great feeling for inside information.

When I finished with that, I watched him for a while, and was happy to see that the poor son of a bitch was closing the sale. Bucky starts to move around a lot, and he takes real fast little steps when he's closing a sale. It's the only sign he shows of being pleased and excited.

He came pitty-pattying up to the office, and I told him I was taking off to look at a 1971 Ford panel truck, which was a lie. I just wanted to get the hell out of there. What I needed was a new sales campaign, like the Wingback Lake Campaign, to get me interested in life once more.

15

When I got out of town, I turned off the road where Sheila Richards and I had driven the day before, and after twenty minutes or a half hour, I came across this little white farmhouse with two antiques signs in the front yard.

I suppose a good salesman always likes a good sales talk now and then, whether he's on the receiving end or the delivery end. You get so you can enjoy it as an art.

That's one reason I stopped: I always like to give a man a chance to sell me something. But also, I had been thinking about what Winslow had said about my office needing a couple pictures. In spite of the elk antlers and the cup of free Marlboros, it *was* pretty barren inside, and a couple pictures *would* brighten things up. Also, my wife is crazy about antiques, and I figured maybe I would find something she would like. Sort of a coming-home present.

I park the car in the driveway, which is bordered by stones that were painted white about ten years ago and are now pretty faded. Then I get out of the car and walk up to the door, but halfway there an old lady comes out to meet me. She is wearing corduroy pants—a pair of man's pants, so far as I could figure—and a man's shirt rolled up above the elbows. Her hair is all screwed up like a briar patch, and she looks so much like a far-gone mental case that I am already halfway sorry I stopped.

She just stares at me as if she thinks I am an intruder. Maybe she has forgotten that there are antiques signs standing in front. Anyway, I remind her, and she nods and says, "What are you interested in, Mister . . . Mister . . ."

"McCoy," I tell her. "I'm interested in some pictures, maybe, if you have some around."

"Oh, I see, Mr. McCoy," she says. "Are you from town?"

I told her I was, although I'm not sure we meant the same one, and she said, "Oh yes, you're the car dealer, aren't you?" Then she asked me what kind of pictures I was interested in. I couldn't answer, because I didn't really know. But this didn't seem to bother her. She kept asking me questions until I was about ready to call it quits. I couldn't see any antiques about anyway, and I was beginning to wonder if maybe she really was crazy.

But she must have gotten a signal that I had had enough, because she suddenly turned and led me down a walk to a little shed in back.

She shoved the door open, and said, "I don't know whether I have anything you'd want, Mr. McCoy, but you can certainly look around."

"Thank you," I said. "Scientists Say Women Live Longer, May Be Healthier."

Inside, there were some dirty old tables and a few bits of glassware and china. On one wall, there were several pictures. One of them was a photograph of some World War I soldiers, another one was a painting of mountains, and still another one was an old print showing a boy leading two cows along a dirt road.

But it was the last one that caught my eye. It was a black-and-white print of Abraham Lincoln, about three feet high by two feet wide. It was a picture I had seen a lot, but it still kind of interested me.

"How much for that one?" I asked her.

"The one of President Lincoln?" she asked.

"That's the one," I said.

"Oh, you can have that for about six dollars. The frame isn't very good."

I gave her six dollars and left with the picture, thinking

it was a shame dumb-ass old Winslow couldn't see it right away.

I felt good driving back to town. I kept thinking about Sheila Richards, and about the picture of Lincoln. I have always admired Lincoln.

Whatever it was, I was feeling pretty good, and when I turned left back into town from the highway and stopped at the first traffic light down by Pennington's Sunoco station, I just idly let my eyes wander around, and I saw the same stupid poster I had seen at breakfast that morning. Right there in the window of Bill Pennington's station. The poster about the hillbilly group called the Hatfield Four.

And then it really hit me. Just like it was waiting for me, or was even part of fate. Because here were two of those silly damn posters still hanging around two weeks after the Hatfield Four had finished playing at the Lewistown Grange Hall.

I pulled my Buick over to the curb, near a corner phone booth, and parked it with its ass sticking halfway over a yellow line. But that wasn't important; what was important was to strike while the iron was hot.

I went up to a little neighborhood grocery and bought a five-pack of Dutch Masters panetelas as an excuse to get some dimes for several phone calls in the booth on the corner.

First I called Dwight Stambough, who owns a record shop downtown, and asked him to look up the Hatfield Four for me and tell me who recorded their work. Dwight told me their company was called T. & G. Productions, and they were located in Nashville. Dwight even gave me their number.

I phoned, charged the call to my business, got the name of the agent of the Hatfield Four, and immediately put in a call for him. His office was also in Nashville.

It was while I was standing there in the booth waiting

for the call to be completed that I saw a brand-new Olds turn the corner. Some skinny, exotic-looking stud with a deep tan and wearing a beret was driving, and Sheila Richards was sitting right next to him. She must have had one cheek of her ass damn near on his leg, she was so close. They were both wearing sunglasses, and I just got a glance at them; but there wasn't any doubt. It was Sheila Richards, the swinging old bitch of Taylor Hall fame, and T. F. Hanaway dictation, and Rex (born Regius) McCoy salesmanship.

Women Found Polyandrous.

In a couple of seconds, they were gone and the number in Nashville gave me a Cincinnati hotel number, where the agent and the Hatfield Four were holing up.

Within another twenty minutes, I had gotten the agent on the phone. He was a man named Gunther, and he had a voice like he had been weaned on stump-hole whiskey. I could tell from several signals here and there that the Hatfield Four weren't being overworked these days. After a lot of double talk and good old-fashioned bullshit, Gunther mentioned that they just might be available in another ten days.

Right then and there I booked the Hatfield Four for the first week in July to play on our lot. What I was thinking of was a great campaign. A chance in a lifetime. A beautiful coincidence. I would have been stupid not to take advantage of a great campaign idea like this.

When I walked back to my car, I got some old envelopes, which had once contained bills, out of the glove compartment, and began to sketch out a sales campaign that would make the Wingback Lake thing practically evaporate by comparison.

First thing I thought of was this radio commercial, with a background of hillbilly music from the Hatfield Four.

Then there would be the sound of rifle shots, a couple

ricochets, and maybe a little yelling and screaming (I wasn't sure about this part yet), and the music would stop, and then this fellow would say, "The Hatfields and the McCoys are AT IT AGAIN!"

The possibilities after that were endless.

I was glad my wife wasn't home. This is the kind of thing that makes her think she's one of the British nobility or something, and her pride and dignity will be damaged forever by her gross, tasteless, flamboyant son of a bitch of a husband.

16

That afternoon I told Buckholz and Cripps about my new sales plan, and they said it was the greatest idea I had ever had.

"Who's the best?" I yelled, and we all kind of stood there and grinned. I took my handkerchief out and wiped a spot off the windshield of a lime-green LTD.

I phoned Altizer's Department Store and ordered by-God, old-fashioned bib overalls and red-checked shirts and straw hats for all of us. Then I tried to think of someplace where I could get some jugs and old-looking rifles or shotguns. I could use an old Damascus-barreled ten gauge I've had lying around, and then there was an ancient Kentucky half-stock in the attic.

For a while I was thinking about buying an old outhouse, if I could find one, and having Perry Wilson haul it in on his truck. We could put it out by the sign that says "McCoy's Used Cars," where it would attract plenty of attention. I considered putting a sign on it, too: "The Don't-Be-Left-Out House!"

I was happy as hell, spending money, using my imagination, spinning my mind off a thousand ideas, building and creating like a crazy son of a bitch. A man can't be happy unless he's building something.

And I like to do things right away. I hate long-range planning and always have. It was only a couple hours back that I had gotten the idea about the Hatfields and the McCoys, and here I had already hired them for a week's engagement and planned my major strategy. I'd been so busy I'd even forgotten to take my picture of Abraham Lincoln out of the back seat of my car.

But right then I did think of it, and took it out. I brought it into the office. Bucky was sitting there with a toothpick in his mouth, watching me. Finally, he said, "Rex, what's 'at?"

"That is a picture of Abraham Lincoln," I told him.

Bucky nodded and thought a minute, while I rummaged around in the desk, looking for some string and a screw to hang it up with.

"What are you going to do with it?" Bucky asked, leaning over to look at it a little closer, where it was standing against the wall.

"I am going to hang it over there beside the elk antlers," I told him. "Local Establishment Needs Sprucing Up."

Bucky looked at the wall and nodded. I slammed the drawer shut, and said, "I can't ever find a goddam thing I want. Didn't we have some string and a couple screws in here someplace?"

"Seems we did, someplace," Bucky said.

But goddam if I could find them, so I went out of the office and headed for La Rue's Hardware, which is only about a hundred and fifty yards down the street from our lot.

Yerby's Gin Mill is only a little farther along the street,

and even though it was still pretty early in the afternoon, I decided to go on over and have a double of Jack Daniel's and maybe bring my boil down to a simmer.

Yerby was having the men's room painted. I recognized one of the painters, because I had sold him a '64 Chevy about five years before.

I drank a J. D. and lighted a Dutch Masters panetela. Suddenly I got this idea for the big sign, so I got out a little notebook I carry around to jot down my inspirations in and wrote:

> CADILLACS COME HIGH,
> VW'S THEY GO LOW:
> OLD REX HAS GOT THE CAR FOR YOU
> NO MATTER WHAT THE DOUGH.

I put this masterpiece back in my pocket, and then, as I sipped at the J. D., I began to wonder if old Sheila baby had given me a dose or something, and who that skinny, tanned stud she was driving around with was. I only wished I could have seen his face. One thing for sure: he was driving a nice car.

I was still elated. I took my wife's postcard out and said, "Yerby, you don't happen to read Spanish, do you?"

Then old Yerby surprised me. He says, "Sure. What you want me to read?"

I handed him the postcard, and Yerby translated as follows:

Dearest:

Spain is simply too beautiful, but I miss you. Tomorrow we are going to the Balearic Islands, and it's just possible that we will get a glimpse of Robert Graves, because we will pass through his village. This card will help you brush up on your Spanish. I still miss you.

So long.

He gives me the card back and I say, "How in the hell did you learn to read Spanish?"

"I was in the Coast Guard in Puerto Rico for a year and a half," Yerby says. "It's an easy language."

I didn't say anything to that, and Yerby added: "After you get used to it."

"What?" I asked him.

"Spanish," he said. "It's easy after you get used to it. You know, get the hang of it. Like anything."

I nodded, and then drank another double J. D. pretty quick, so that when I walked out the door, I seemed to be walking on an air cushion about four inches thick. Which is not a bad way to walk, I've always said.

I went on down the street a little farther to the Western Union office, and went in and told Lloyd Ripple I wanted to send a telegram to my wife. I gave him her hotel address, and then wrote:

Dear Mother,
Dealer Sends Greetings Bob, Rex.

Lloyd Ripple looked at what I'd written for a minute, and then he said, "None of my business, Rex, but don't you want to check this? I mean, didn't you leave a word out?"

I glanced at it lying there on the counter, and said, "Nope, that's the way I wanted it."

Lloyd said, "Okay, but it wouldn't cost you anything to add the word 'to' there, so that it would read, 'Dealer Sends Greetings *to* Bob.' That *is* what you meant, isn't it?"

"Nope. It's just the way I want it."

"Okay, if that's the way you want it."

"That's it," I told him.

He shrugged and turned around. But then my curiosity got the better of me, and I said, "Have you ever heard of any goddam body named Robert Graves?"

Lloyd frowned and shook his head.

"He lives in Spain," I said.

"Can't say I ever have," Lloyd said.

"Well, that's who I am telling her to say hello to. Whoever he is. She says tomorrow she might get a glimpse of him. Or maybe that would be today. Whenever she sent the goddam card."

I kind of rambled on like this for a while, because I was a little bit drunk and I felt like talking.

Finally I said, "Miniskirts Up; Maxis Down," and went outside, where I saw Clendon Metzger's miraculous Buick parked in the A & P parking lot. Then I went on uptown to Altizer's to see if they had gotten my order for the bib overalls and shirts right.

I was beginning to feel like hell. I was walking past the sock counter in Altizer's, as a matter of fact, when I had this spell I had gotten a few times lately. Everything got real dark and kind of unreal. And things seemed very far away and tiny. I mean my hand looked like the petal of a flower and the girl at the sock counter looked like she was wet, but on fire and standing at the bottom of a deep well.

Something happened to the sound system in my head, too. Everybody sounded like they were far away, sealed off in another room or something.

Naturally, I hadn't told my wife. She would've nagged me to go to the doctor, but I hate the goddam doctors. If ever a man wants the dignity of privacy, it's when he's sick or having some kind of weakness or attack like this.

I could tell the salesgirl was looking at me funny, and she asked me a question, but I couldn't answer her.

Finally it all passed away and I walked away from her. My shirt was soaked with sweat, but I was chilly. I loosened my string tie and went out into the sunlight and put my sunglasses on. The sunlight felt good on my bald head, but it was remote, like the heat of a register on your hand.

Over at the A & P, Mother Metzger was getting in the

car, and old Clendon was doddering along behind her, counting some change in his hand, it looked like. They didn't see me.

I walked slow and steady back to the lot, putting my feet down like I was laying fortunetelling cards on a table. Finally, I got to my car and climbed in without saying anything to Cripps, who was smoking a Marlboro from the cup on my desk and scratching some kind of travel sticker off a windshield. Then I drove home.

There was a hammock out in back and I went there and lay down a while, keeping my eyes closed and listening to the birds singing and fluttering as thick as the thorns in the honey locust trees we have in back. After a while, I began to feel a little better. But I lay there and half slept and half thought morbid thoughts about things.

One of which was my father, who had died young—at the age of forty-five—of pneumonia during World War II. I got the news in the South Pacific. Harry Biddle was still alive then. This was before Iwo.

I also thought about how many other people I had survived. Not only all the Marines that were killed around me in World War II, but others as well . . . my mother, and a pretty girl in high school who died of encephalitis, and a friend in Rotary who killed himself with a captured German Luger only a year or so back . . . and the strange deaths, like Ben Sanderson, who electrocuted himself doing house repairs, and a really strange, screwed-up jasper I had gone to high school with named Jonathan Neil, who was killed in the collapse of the Silver Bridge across the Ohio River. They never found his body. And an old lady named Miss Grace Wimsett, who, believe it or not, strangled to death on a perch bone. She was a close friend of my grandmother's, and she did beautiful needlework up to the very day of her death.

There is a time you reach in your life when you have known more people who are dead than living.

All these morbid thoughts swam around in my mind for a while, but then I began to feel better and eventually I dozed off, with my leg beginning to ache . . . which is a good sign, because it carries a vague ache most of the time and acts as sort of a barometer for the rest of my body. It's like the comfort the tug of gravity must be to the astronauts when they come back to earth.

I woke up about four o'clock and realized I had forgotten all about getting the screws and string at La Rue's Hardware, so Abraham Lincoln's picture was probably still leaning against the wall beside my desk. Maybe it was turning black in the presence of Bucky and Cripps.

A soft breeze was coming up over the hill, smelling of freshly cut grass from one of the yards down below and the green leaves of the woods that separate our houses. I could hear the power mower still gnawing away down there, probably at the Paulys or the Bennetts.

This was a night we stayed open, so I got up and rinsed my face off with cold water from the tap. That made me feel still better—almost a hundred per cent—so I went out to dinner and ate a turkey salad sandwich and a bowl of canned chicken gumbo soup and a cup of tea, which settles my stomach.

Then I went back to the lot and found two pamphlets and a note Professor Winslow had left on my desk, plus another note in Cripps's handwriting saying I had had two calls while I was gone—one from a colored man named Blivens, who was interested in buying a VW, and one from Miss Richards.

Winslow's note said, "How about it? With your gifts, you could do something in this regard."

The pamphlets were titled *The Need for Federal Reap-*

portionment and *Eight Errors in the Conservative Establishment*. I tossed them aside.

I called Blivens' number, but nobody answered. Then I called Sheila's number, and she asked why she hadn't heard from me. She asked if I was mad at her or something, and I told her I wasn't.

But I could tell she wasn't convinced. I didn't say anything about not feeling so good that afternoon or seeing her out driving with another man. So we didn't communicate, as Professor Homer Winslow would have said. There were a couple long silences when we just kind of leaned into the phone and breathed, and then finally I said, "New Cure for Piles, Hemorrhoids," and she made an irritated noise, and then we said good-by and hung up.

I rummaged through the drawer again, and found some heavy white paper and a Magic Marker. I spread the paper out on the desk, and printed a sign, which read:

SALESMANSHIP IS CHARISMA

When I finished it, I got some Scotch Tape and fastened it to the wall right near the desk. I could almost see Bucky come in and stand there looking at it, switching his toothpick back and forth in his mouth. Then I could hear him asking, "What's 'at?"

God knows how I would ever explain it to him.

A couple minutes later, I took off and got some little three-quarter-inch number-seven woodscrews and some twine, which we ought to keep around the office anyway, since we always have a hundred uses for it. When I got back, I hung up the picture. When Cripps came in, he looked at it a minute out of his cocked eyes, and said, "Honest Abe."

I nodded and looked at the picture, too.

"They don't make them like that any more," Cripps said.

"No," I said, "they don't."

Old Cripps didn't even see the charisma sign I'd put up. Not even when he went over to the cup and helped himself to a fistful of Marlboros.

17

One thing I have omitted from my account of that afternoon is coming across my brother, Randall, who I haven't mentioned yet. It was right after seeing Clendon Metzger and Mother, and right before the business in Altizer's. I happened to glance across the street, and there was Randall, standing with his back to me, looking in the window of a clothing store. He had had his hair cut, so that for the first time in about fifteen years he didn't look like a medieval monk; but there was no mistaking him.

I stood there for a couple seconds, looking at his back, and then I was aware that he wasn't about to turn around to confront me brother to brother, because he was already looking at me. He was staring at my reflection in the store window. It was pretty far away, but I am certain that was exactly what he was doing.

A couple seconds later, I moseyed on down the street, thinking that this was a typical encounter with the poor, screwed-up son of a bitch. First of all, it's always a surprise for me to see him out on the streets at all. At least in this part of town. But even when I do happen to run into him, we sometimes manage to turn the other way and mutually pretend we're not there.

Now that I've finally mentioned Randall, I'm going to try explaining what kind of person he is; and that is going to be hard, but I'll be as honest as I can.

First of all, he's a year and two months older than me, and he is about the nearest thing to a by-God, full-time lunatic you can find outside the walls of a mental institution. That reflection-in-the-window business is a fair sample.

But then, he's always been odd. We looked enough alike to be twins until along about junior high school, when Randall started getting fat. From then on, we got more and more different every year.

I was always full of piss and vinegar, and Randall was always very lazy, physically, and quiet and unobtrusive. We were as different as day and night. I played football in college, but Randall didn't play a damned thing, not even a trombone, and he dropped out of college after a year.

All the son of a bitch did was read. Mostly literature and philosophy and history books. In a way, I suppose he was smart as hell, but anybody would admit he's kind of a freak. Years ago, when they had these quiz shows on TV, and people all thought they were honest, I said to myself, Now there's a chance for Randall to really be successful.

But of course he didn't do anything about it; and it wasn't actually any surprise to me that he didn't. I couldn't really have imagined old Randall up there in front of a TV camera, before a nationwide audience. By that time, he had really gone eccentric. He was cutting his own hair in a kind of ridge all the way around his forehead. Like Moe of the Three Stooges. This was to save money for books. He was wearing glasses, and his eyes bothered him so much—or maybe it was his nerves—that he was always screwing up his face and making a strange little humming noise, which I think you were supposed to interpret as clearing his throat.

By that time, too, he was about sixty or seventy pounds heavier than I was, and his wife, Betty, had to practically throw a tantrum to get him out of the dirty sweatshirts he was always wearing.

Betty and Randall got married shortly after my wife and I did. Betty went to work right away as a telephone operator, and she hasn't quit since. I suppose they might have had kids if things had been different, but Betty has always had her hands full with Randall. And, of course, with her job.

They live in a dumpy little frame house on the cruddy edge of town, and their back yard goes all the way back, about five hundred feet. Now here's where things get really interesting.

Fifty feet back of the house is an old shed about the size of a three-car garage. There are windows all around this shed, only they haven't been washed for about ten years, so you can't see anything but big flat panes of gray dust. The shed was built by a man named Theoluce Adams, Randall says, back in 1892. He built it as an experimental greenhouse. (Randall says that Theoluce's name means "Light of God"; I wouldn't know about that, but if anyone asks, it's okay with me.)

Anyway, Theoluce built this greenhouse of his with a solid roof—just like any kind of structure—but he put large mirrors outside the windows. He had them on hinges at the bottoms, slanting outwards from the top and hanging by thin chains, so that they could be adjusted to catch the maximum sunlight at any hour of the day. On each wall there was a master lever connected to all the chains of the mirrors for that wall. Theoluce could stand there and adjust the pitch for the whole window on the hour, so that his plants could catch the light available. He felt this gave him a control over the light in such a way that his name was justified.

Theoluce died under mysterious circumstances shortly after World War I, leaving the long planting tables standing in the shed. Randall says that when he and Betty first bought the house, there were still a few broken pots and clumps of dirt on the tables. But the mirrors had all been broken by vandals, and torn from the chains.

Randall didn't utilize the shed in any way Theoluce Adams could have imagined. Instead, he put about fifteen hundred whiskey bottles along the planting tables. By now, he must have something like four thousand. He drinks whiskey (Old Log Cabin and Echo Spring bourbon, most of the time), and he buys whiskey bottles everywhere he can, digs them out of garbage cans in the back alleys about town . . . he collects them.

Let me tell you, it is a strange sight to step inside and see four thousand whiskey bottles standing upright in jagged rows along these waist-high tables. They are all clouded with dust now; and the light isn't too good—although there are a few naked yellow bulbs fixed in ceiling sockets.

Lately, Randall has been having trouble with vandals who break the windows and even get inside sometimes and break a few bottles. God knows why he would mind, except I guess he looks upon them as *his,* and nobody likes to have his own property damaged. Even if it is a bunch of goddam worthless whiskey bottles.

But this is only the beginning of Randall's kingdom. There is a path that goes right past the shed and then dips down to a little gulley that has water in it most of the year. Then it joins with a little swinging footbridge, which the same screwball, Theoluce, built back near the turn of the century.

Then you go over the footbridge, up a steep bank and through a thick line of brush and trees, and by the time you reach the top, you are on a flat area, which is nothing but a big vacant field full of briars and poison ivy and wild timothy, and a few hickory, locust and elm saplings here and there. There is also, underneath all the dead weeds, a railroad spur that was discontinued about 1934. This is still Randall's property, and on the spur there are two old Pullman cars—vintage about 1910—and a discarded caboose, which all belong to Randall. He paid a hundred and fifty dollars for the caboose right after World War II, and about three or four hundred for the two Pullman cars—although I don't know the exact amount for these.

Anyway, these cars are now filled to the ceilings with old books, a little hand printing press, and a lot of miscellaneous junk, which Randall has collected for as long as I can remember. The poor nutty son of a bitch goes back there to his railroad cars at about nine o'clock every morning, when Betty goes off to the telephone company, and plays with his books. I don't know what all he does with them. He reads them, of course, and makes file cards for them, and writes letters and takes notes and talks to himself and looks at pictures. Sometimes he prints his own little pamphlets, with his little hand press, on such exciting subjects as the book collection of J. Pierpont Shithead or the kinds of neckties Ambrose Bierce wore or the idea of private property among the American Indians, which he is also an expert on.

I've been back there a couple times, and believe me, it's odd. The books are stuck in shelves he's made, but they're also piled in stacks clean up to the ceilings, as I mentioned. But here and there old Randall has hung Navy-surplus hammocks filled with dusty old letters and magazines and books, and even an artificial leg sticking out of one of them with a ripped and torn woman's silk stocking on it. In one of the Pullman cars the seats are torn out; but the other one still has its seats, all cluttered with boxes, beer cans, old wine bottles, suitcases, magazines, advertising brochures, flowerpots, rags, shoes, an old rocker, women's hats from the Gay Nineties . . . and of course books.

Randall's got a roll-top desk in the caboose, and he refers to this as his office. He wears a green eyeshade and chews tobacco and spits in a spittoon by the desk. There's a potbellied stove he burns coal in when it's chilly outside, and everything looks about fifty years out of date. Outside, the milkweed and wild timothy and bull thistles grow as high as a man's shoulders. Randall won't let Betty go near the three cars, which he calls his domain.

Another thing is that Randall has these delusions of grandeur concerning his books. I suppose he has twenty thousand of the goddam things back there in those railroad coaches and the caboose. And in his own screwy way, he has them catalogued. At least, Betty says he's able to find almost anything he wants.

About every two or three months, Randall has another will made, or at least codicils for his will. His lawyer is none other than T. F. Hanaway. Randall's got this idea that his books are treasures of humanity, and that the whole world is waiting to hear what the last dispensation will be.

Since he buys books and old magazines and letters all the time (he's got forty letters of Ambrose Bierce, although you ask ten people in the street who Ambrose Bierce is, and eight of them, if they're men, will answer that he played for the Detroit Lions about ten years ago, along with Cloyse Box, Dorne Dibble and Doak Walker), he figures that the will has to be kept up to date. Think of how many people wouldn't be able to sleep if they knew that one of Ambrose Bierce's letters wasn't accounted for in Randall McCoy's will!

Eccentric Collector Leads Hermit's Life.

You can imagine how my wife feels about him. She wouldn't be caught dead in Randall's and Betty's house; but then I sometimes tell her they probably don't feel too terribly deprived by her absence.

Of course, I feel sorry for Betty in a way. She is about five feet tall and weighs something like ninety-five pounds. She has big tired eyes and a wrinkled neck, even though her build isn't too bad at all. She's eight years older than Randall, and she wouldn't step on an ant, if she could help it. She has a beautiful, ladylike voice that sounds even better over the phone. I get her sometimes on a long-distance call, and I always give her a bad time, along with a few last-minute bulletins, like "Man Abandons Spouse, Self." (She knows who it is.) She's so kind and sensitive, it isn't normal. It's almost like she was asking for it. When you see a frail and sensitive little woman like that married to a buffalo like Randall, you really wonder. Of course, nobody *told* the poor dumb thing to get tied up with somebody like Randall.

She spends all her time working and keeping house and watching television. If anybody criticizes Randall (with the mistaken notion that they are somehow taking up for Betty), she gets very precise and cold and indignant, and tells them politely to go to hell, with lady words, and mentions that Randall has a book in his possession that is worth over fifteen hundred dollars.

When she said this to me once, I told her to have old Randall bring it down to the lot, and I might take it in as a trade on a 1958 Pontiac wagon I'd had around the lot for a couple months. She just stared at me, then, and Randall just kind of blinked behind his glasses. I don't think he even heard me, let alone caught on to the joke.

One more thing about Randall: I said he was a lunatic, but that isn't exactly true. The way I see it, he acts the way he does because he *wants* to. You can't make me believe he doesn't know how screwy he seems to other people. He's pretty sharp, in spite of everything. But he's just a bug on collecting things. Books, especially.

Of course, he must be a little bit off to *want* to do what he does, so maybe he's screwy after all. I guess it's what Homer Winslow would call a problem in semantics.

One thing sure, though: my brother Randall is a problem, no matter how you consider it.

I sometimes go for weeks at a time without seeing him, or even thinking of the poor bastard.

18

When the Hatfield Four came, we were ready. For ninety dollars, I had a five-foot-high platform built to hold them. I wrote up a little deal with Pete Wister, who is a contractor about town, that he would build a platform that would stand there as long as the Hatfield Four were engaged. When I was through using it, Pete would tear it down and use the lumber again. The lumber and materials were all his; the structure itself was mine. He owned the body; I owned the less expensive part—the soul, you might say.

I had banners put all around the lot, and a special set of spotlights to focus on the platform. Cripps has a brother who is a good electrician, so I left all the wiring up to him (it was pretty elementary, but I knew one of the Hatfield Four played an electric guitar sometimes, and then I figured the spots might take a different hook-up).

There was a big, eight-by-fifteen-foot sign at the front, showing two old hillbillies glaring at each other. They both had jugs and guns and long whiskers; and then at the top, there was lettering that said, just like the radio commercial, "The Hatfields and the McCoy's are at it again!"

The guy who did the sign only put one exclamation mark on it, but I made him add a couple extra ones. I also made him put in three or four "bangs" in the background, and little cartoon puffs of smoke. Outside of the radio commercials, the sign—complete with two spotlights shining on it—was the most expensive thing of all; the son of a bitch cost me two hundred forty.

When the overalls and bandannas came from Altizer's, it was a kind of a shock. That first evening, I almost considered changing my mind. First there was Cripps, with his cocked eyes and his sick complexion, and then there was old 340-pound Bucky, in a pair of overalls that had enough material in them to clothe a whole Boy Scout troop. I had been wrong—Bucky didn't look any better in clothes that fit him than he did in those tight goddam pants he was always wearing.

But the old Buck came through. He seemed happier than usual, and for the first half hour of the opening he kept dodging behind cars and shooting at me with his finger, like some kid. Naturally, he was just acting up and horsing around, but you could tell he was kind of enjoying himself, too.

Well, I let him frolic. I didn't have the heart to let on how ridiculous the poor brainless son of a bitch looked, and the Hatfield Four hadn't arrived on stage yet. Cripps seldom said anything to Bucky, good or bad, so there was probably no way on God's earth for Buckholz to find out that he looked about as much like a hillbilly as Jackie Gleason or Winston Churchill.

At first there weren't any customers, and I figured that even after they arrived, the Hatfield Four wouldn't bring too many in for the first hour or two. People have to get warmed up. Bucky and Cripps and I had put on our overalls about six-thirty, but the Hatfield Four weren't due to show up until eight. That would leave about an hour and a half of daylight. Then they'd play until eleven, with our Husky Grip Paper Mate ball-point pens, which I keep my boys well supplied with, scratching along in counterpoint. At least this is what I was hoping. The fact is, I had spent a lot of money on this thing, and already I was a little curious about the outcome.

At ten minutes till eight, Bucky said, "Shouldn't they be here by now?"

I told him it wasn't actually time yet, and Bucky said yes, but it would take them a few minutes to set up their equipment.

That was true, and I began to wonder where in the hell they were. I had met the four of them, along with their agent, Gunther, that morning. We had drunk a cup of coffee together at the motel where they were staying.

When eight o'clock came and they still hadn't shown up, I went to the phone and dialed the motel. Gunther answered in that gravel voice of his after about ten rings.

"Hatfields McCoys to Clash Again," I said. "And No Shit."

"Is this Mr. McCoy?"

"The one and only," I said. "Where is everybody?"

"Can't answer for *everybody,*" Gunther said, barking a laugh into the telephone.

When I didn't laugh or say anything, Gunther got a reasoning sound in his voice and said, "Look here, Mr. McCoy. We'll be over there as soon as we can line up Little Hermie. Right? As soon as we can line him up, we'll be right over there. It ain't hardly more than a—what—ten-minute drive? Eight minutes?"

"What in the hell are you trying to pull?" I asked him.

"Little Hermie," he said. "You know, the little sport-job fella. You met him just this morning. He's the one with the real high voice—falsetto, they call it—who's always yelling out, 'Don't leave me out here all *alone!*' "

When I didn't say anything at all, Gunther said, "You know something? People are *crazy* about that little son of a bitch."

"Well, where in the hell *is* he?" I asked.

"Well, sir, that I can't rightly say. Oh, no sweat, Mr. McCoy. Little Hermie's around here *someplace*. That you can be sure of. Yes, sir, he's around here *someplace!*"

He broke off and yelled to somebody in the background, "Merle, any sign of Little Hermie yet?"

I heard a mumble in the background, and then Gunther said—like he was still talking to the other fellow and giving him comfort—"Well, that's all right. He'll show up in a few minutes. Just like he always does."

I heard the other fellow say something like "Shit," but I couldn't be sure.

"Look here," I said. "I've got over three thousand worth of advertising in you people, and, by God, you better get on over here, and I mean quick." That wasn't strictly true about the three thousand, but I figured exaggeration was Gunther's native tongue.

"Mr. McCoy," Gunther said, "I want to tell you something in confidence. Now, you're a man of the world, I can see that. Right? I told Merle this morning; I said, 'Merle, that man McCoy has been around.' "

He turned his head away, but I could still hear him all right. "Merle, isn't that what I said this morning?"

I didn't hear any answer at all to that, and I figured Merle wasn't co-operating. I wasn't sure whether Merle was the Hatfield of the group or not. I had dealt all the way through with this whiskey-throated son of a bitch named Gunther, and when I met the four artists, as Gunther referred to them, that morning, I hadn't picked up on their names. Although I do remember there was this little pint-sized fellow with kind of wild eyes and real long sideburns and slicked-down hair. That must have been Little Hermie.

"Never mind the bullshit," I told him.

Gunther came back to the subject then—at least to the subject as he saw it. "Mr. McCoy," he said, "this is in the strictest confidence. I'm going to tell you something about Little Hermie which, if it once got out to the world at large, would ruin the life of a wonderful little guy."

"What are you talking about?" I asked him.

"What I am talking about is this: Little Hermie isn't exactly acting."

"What?"

"Exactly. Little Hermie isn't exactly acting when he uses the falsetto."

"Just what are you talking about?" I said.

"Exactly what I said, Mr. McCoy. When Little Hermie cries out, 'Don't leave me out here all *alone!*' everybody in the audience gets a great laugh out of it—I tell you, they're *crazy* about that kid!—but what I'm saying, Mr. McCoy, is this: Little Hermie isn't actually, one hundred per cent acting."

"Gunther," I said, "I don't know what you're talking about. What's more, how do you like this for a headline: Press Agent Slain by Irate Car King?"

"Anxiety, Mr. McCoy. Arrested development. That's what."

"What in the *hell* is what?"

"I mean to confide in you, in the strictest confidence, that Little Hermie gives that cry from the heart. I mean to confide in you that Little Hermie hasn't completely growed up in every way, if you grasp my meaning, and when he gives forth with that call, it comes from the heart. I mean to confide that the poor little son of a bitch is a child at heart, and we have to take care of him like a goddam kid."

"Well, where *is* he?" I asked. "And why are you telling *me* all this bullshit for?"

"What I am confiding in you for," Gunther said in a low voice, "is to convey to you the simple fact that Little Hermie could not of gone very far. He could not of strayed far from the rest of us, because he has this secret and morbid anxiety about being left all alone someplace. You know, like a poor little goddam kid. Lost."

"Gunther," I said, "you and the Hatfield Four better haul-ass over here right away, or I will slap a lawsuit on you for breach of contract, and I will sue you for everything, including your goddam satin pants and the silver braid on your shirts and the brilliantine on your hair, and the . . ."

"Wait!" Gunther interrupted. "Just wait a minute! Hold on!"

There was such a frantic sound in his voice that I stopped talking and did wait.

Then, in a quiet and very calm voice, Gunther said, "Little Hermie has just come back. Everything is all right, and we'll be over there in—what—ten minutes?"

"By God you had better be," I told him. Then I hung up.

Out on the lot, Bucky was going through his dance, taking a lot of tiny, nervous steps in front of a jasper with a beard. Only, the jasper was a college student, not a hillbilly. Somehow, you can always tell.

Well, how about that Bucky? Making a sale already, and going through his victory waddle. And without the benefit of the Hatfield and McCoy business or that old riverboat gambler, Gunther, or silent Merle. Even without Little Hermie, who didn't ever want to be left alone.

19

They were exactly fourteen minutes late. Gunther appeared wearing a Chinese-red silk shirt and a silver string tie. He had a face like a bloodhound with an eighty-year hangover, which exactly suited his voice. He was well over six feet tall, about six five, I would say, and he had long, tired, sloping shoulders and about forty pounds of gut slipped down comfortably below his belt, where it wouldn't be in the way. There must have been about a thousand wrinkles in his face, and his eyes folded down on the outsides, giving him that hound-dog look. He must have been somewhere over sixty years old, and he had a boiled complexion and a nose like Harris tweed.

I would not have trusted the bastard to light my cigar, and it irritated me that he would show up wearing a string tie, which has been kind of my personal trademark about town for years.

Merle was almost the same height, but a lot younger—about thirty-five—and better built. He had wide, hard-looking jaws and little bitty black eyes right close together. He was wearing about six big, expensive-looking rings on both hands, and I found out later that Merle hardly ever said a word. He was quieter than Cripps with a bellyache, which is quiet. Merle's last name was Ciphers, and he played the bass viol. Gunther later told me Merle had a wife and nine kids back in Tennessee. Gunther said he figured he was so dumb he didn't know what was causing all the kids; but then he wasn't sure, because Merle had been with the group only three years, and Gunther had yet to hear a complete sentence. For all he knew, Merle might be a genius. Only he kind of doubted it.

Billy Joe Spangler came up to Merle's chin, but he was about twice as wide. He had curly black hair and was the fattest one hillbilly I ever hope to see; looking at him, I realized that Bucky wasn't quite as ridiculous as I had thought. Billy Joe played the electric guitar and doubled on the twelve-string banjo.

The third member was the Hatfield. His first name was Jimmy. Ron Bowzer from the newspaper came down, and Jimmy Hatfield and I squared off against each other for a couple gag shots. We were right up there on stage, and when I stepped back from the second shot, I stepped on Gunther's foot. He had somehow managed to get in the picture, although for the life of me, I couldn't tell you how. He moved fast for a man his age.

Jimmy Hatfield was normal-sized, with long hair that was as limp as rubber bands and kept flying down in his face. He played lead guitar, and he wore glasses. He not only *was* the leader of the group, he let everyone know it—except maybe Gunther, who was kind of domineering himself, in his own oily way. Jimmy Hatfield spent half the evening with his hand on the mike, and whenever Little Hermie sang out, "Don't leave me out here all *alone!*" Jimmy would grab the microphone and grin and say, "How about that, folks. Let's hear it for the little fella!"

The first two or three times he said that, I about vomited, because there weren't over a dozen people in the whole lot. Maybe Jimmy couldn't see well enough through his glasses to know the audience hadn't gathered yet.

Little Hermie was the fourth member of the group. He played the mandolin. You could tell there was something wrong with him just by watching. He was always rolling his eyes to the side and nervously licking his lips. When they first came up, Merle lifted him like a little child and put him on the platform, and Little Hermie reached around and offered his hand to help Merle up, but Merle vaulted the five feet with only one hand. Then Little Hermie showed his muscle and strutted. It was obvious they had played together a long time, these fellows. A cornball audience would have laughed at their entrance, but of course it was too early for any kind of audience at our place.

Well, Colorful Quartet Takes Over Local Lot, and this was sure as hell a motley crew. But I'll tell you: when they started to play, that was something else! I don't have any particular liking for hillbilly music, but these four odd-ball bastards made our old car lot jump with joy one minute, and melt with schmaltzy tenderness the next.

Old Gunther stayed around a while. He stood there beside me for twenty minutes or a half hour, while the boys were winding up. He was chewing on a Roi-Tan cigar, and his arms were crossed comfortably on top of his belly as he watched and listened. But it was all a business with him; you could tell. When Little Hermie first cut loose with "Don't leave me out here all *alone!*" old Gunther moved sideways, without turning his gaze from the platform, and stepped on my foot. He excused himself, and I told him it was all right.

"I just wanted to tell you," he said, "that they certainly do love the little son of a bitch!"

This was kind of strange, because, as I said, there was hardly anybody on the lot as yet, and there hadn't been so much as a peep out of any of them when Little Hermie first cut loose.

Later on, though, people got in the swing of things, and you could tell they liked it and were getting in the spirit. Every twenty minutes or so, I'd get up on the platform and talk through the microphone about some specials we were offering. Sometimes I'd make history right there and cut the price of a car by fifty or a hundred bucks, and point to Bucky or Cripps and shout: "There's a hillbilly right there that'll let you have that car at the price I just mentioned!"

And it was a damn good evening. Cripps sold three cars, a '69 Impala, a '70 VW, and a Dodge convertible—'68, I think; and Bucky sold four cars (although one was a deal that had been hanging for about three weeks), and I sold nine. So help me. I didn't even try. It seemed like every time I stepped off the platform, somebody was tugging at my sleeve, wanting me to take their money.

They must have figured that any car old Rex sold them would *have* to be something special, something superdependable and *right!*

Naturally, I obliged them. The customer is boss, and all that. Especially when the moon is full and there are sunspots, or some damn thing, and the Hatfield Four are filling the world with excitement.

My charisma was really turned on loud that evening.

I have never been in a better mood in my whole life. It wasn't just selfish, because I was glad as hell to see old Cripps (who has the personality of a catfish with athlete's foot) and old playboy, third-of-a-ton Bucky make out so well. I was so happy, I would have given my nine sales to them, and still I would have been glad. Of course I didn't, because you can't just *give* something to a man. Above everything else, he's got to have pride, and that means he knows he's earned what he gets.

Most of my feeling so good really had to do with the success of my plan. People just came around the same as if the Hatfield Four and I were the Pied Piper. They just laid their goddam heads on the block that night and asked us to chop them off.

I have mentioned how slow things started, but I haven't mentioned how the dam suddenly burst. Old Gunther came around about ten-fifteen, and I asked him how many people he guessed were on the lot right then. The Hatfield Four were going like mad, and Little Hermie was cutting loose with the "out here alone" business about twice a song. Jimmy and fat Billy Joe Spangler would team up with a duet every now and then, and sometimes Little Hermie would join in with his sad-ass falsetto. Or maybe one of them would give a solo.

Anyway, when I asked Gunther how many he figured were on the lot right that instant, the old dog lifts his head, sniffs and turns all around.

"About a hundred and seventy," he said. "Maybe a hundred seventy-five."

Since there was nothing in it for him, I figured I could believe what he said. Right from the start, I didn't trust that fellow. I didn't trust his winning ways.

Gunther took off right after that, and the Hatfield boys were still going strong. I was sitting there, kind of basking in the success of the evening and watching Bucky and Cripps work. I couldn't have been more proud and happy for the silly bastards if they had been a couple of kids—my own sons, even. Although they're both too old for that.

Along about eleven-thirty, Jimmy motioned to me and I told them to cut off for the evening. They had given me an extra half hour because they were late. Only half a dozen people were left around the lot. Once they start to leave, it's like a mysterious signal in a herd of dumb beasts, and before you know it, you're all alone, counting up the receipts.

I went into the office and began doing just that. Bucky and Cripps came in, too, and Bucky cried out: "Who's number one?" And Cripps shouted, "Big Mac!" Then they did a little dance together, like a couple chorus girls, they were so happy. Believe me, not very many human beings have had the opportunity of witnessing a performance like that—Bucky and Cripps, dressed like hillbillies, doing a leg-kicking dance with their arms around each other's shoulders.

I told them they could take off, after that, and Old Rex would tie everything together for the night. So they left. Bucky switched out the floodlights, and both of them walked together in the darkness down to where their cars were parked. It was about twelve-fifteen then.

After I had worked for about five or ten minutes, I got to laughing again. It was one of my goddam little spells, like those dizzy spells. I just sat there in the semidark office and laughed until I thought I was going to fall off the chair. Then I took my Scripto out of the drawer, and a sheet of white cardboard, and printed, "This one won't cost you much more than a big smile from your wife!" I went out and put it in the windshield of a '69 Plymouth Fury. Then I changed my mind, and shifted it to the 1970 Torino I had bought in Columbus a while back.

After this, I began to think of a nightcap up at Yerby's. And before the echoes from this thought had died away, I heard the phone ring in the office. It was Sheila Richards.

"I've got to talk to you," she said.

"What made you think you could catch me here?" I asked her.

"Oh," she said, "I thought you'd be there, working late. I was on the lot at about ten-thirty."

"I didn't see you," I said. "But I guess it was pretty crowded along about ten-thirty."

"I noticed." She paused for a second. "I was there with my husband," she said. "But we kind of stayed on the edge most of the time. And we didn't stay long."

"Your husband?"

"Yes. That's what I wanted to talk with you about. Part of it, anyway."

The laughing was all gone out of me by this time. I took a couple breaths and tried to collect my thoughts. As hard as I had worked all day, I didn't seem to be tired at all. Obviously, I was still keyed up.

"Phil wants to buy me a car," she said then.

"Who?"

"Phil. My husband."

"Oh. That's my boy's name is why I asked. But it's a common name."

"Yes. He was looking at that green Corvette you have next to the street."

"Yes," I said. "That one's a real cream puff."

"I might have known you'd say something like that."

"Now what do you mean by that?"

"I mean, can't you ever forget about *selling* and those crazy things you *say?* That's what I mean."

"I see."

I looked through the window, but I couldn't see the new sign I'd put on the Torino.

"Well," she said, "since you don't want to talk to me . . ."

"Sheila, it isn't that," I told her. "I mean, where could we *talk?* Didn't you say your husband was in town?"

"Yes, he's in town, but he's out of town now. Not only that, we're separated."

I thought about this for a couple seconds, and then she said, "He's come into a lot of money all of a sudden."

"Say," I said, "that sounds great."

"Oh, it is in a way, I suppose."

"What do you mean by that?"

"I can't talk to you like this. Phil's staying with some friends, so he doesn't know if I go out or not. Besides, as I just said, we're separated."

"Well, as I said before, it's so late. I mean, I'd love to see you, but where . . ."

"Is your wife back from Spain yet?"

That one stopped me. And naturally I saw immediately what she was up to, but I didn't know what to say. I have always tried to keep my screwing around away from my wife. I suppose everybody draws the line somewhere, and I had always liked to think I would draw the line at bringing a woman into the house—into *her* house—when my wife was away.

"Well," I said, "I'll tell you what. Let's see . . . you don't have a car, so I'll . . ."

"Yes I do."

"You have a car?"

"Yes. Phil let me borrow his. It's a new Oldsmobile."

"How long has your husband been in town?" I asked her.

"Oh, since right after we saw each other last. You know."

She was right. I knew. So that was the skinny, tanned, foreign-looking fellow she had been driving with that day.

There was nothing else to say, so we hung up, and I lit a cigar and sat there in the half-lighted office, waiting for her. As I waited, I began to think of that postcard in Spanish. If I have ever seen a fully premeditated breakdown in communication, that was it. The more I thought about it, the more indignant I got.

So that when Sheila finally came up, and the headlights of her new Olds flashed across the back wall, the elk antlers and the picture of Abraham Lincoln, I had made up my mind.

I walked up to the car, and when she slid out, I said, "Thousands Flee Flood. Come on. We'll get in my car."

"Where are we going?" she asked me.

"To my house. We can talk there. There's nobody about."

She hesitated a second, then she reached in her car and got her purse.

"Will it be all right here?" she asked.

"Sure," I said. "Nobody would steal a car from old King McCoy's lot. You'd better believe it."

With that, I led her over to my car and we got in. When I turned on the ignition, the radio went on. It was music, and Sheila started crying into a handkerchief.

"Fasten your seat belt," I told her. "You can cry later."

She looked up at me like I had slapped her face.

"After you tell me all about it," I said.

"Oh," she said.

By that time, we were gliding past Yerby's place. The lights were on inside, and it was probably doing a pretty good late business. But it looked like I was going to be doing my drinking elsewhere.

20

The first thing I did was get out a fresh fifth of Jack Daniel's, Green Label, a pitcher of water and a tray of ice. Like always, I got my hands cold and wet. I noticed the front drapes were drawn, so the neighbors across the street wouldn't be entertained, if they were still awake.

Sheila just sat there on the edge of the sofa, with her legs diagonally to the side and snug together, the nice way women like to sit. When I handed her a drink, she held it in both hands and sipped at it. Her surprised-looking eyes were red from crying, but she seemed calmed down now. More than calm; she seemed comfortable.

"I needed this," she said. "You don't know how it's been."

"You mean with your husband?"

She nodded. "His mother died and left him all this money. He wants me to come back with him."

"And you don't want to," I said.

She took a long drink and shook her head no. Actually, she shook her head no while she was still drinking from the glass.

"For one thing," she said, "he's crazy. Absolutely out of his mind. I could never go back to him. I don't think I love him any more. Not exactly."

I didn't say anything, and a couple seconds later, Sheila said, "Look." She held up her arm and showed me some bruises on the inside of her upper arm. "That's where he grabbed me. I've got others, too."

I still didn't know what to say, because she reminded me a little bit of the way my wife is always showing me bruises, resentfully pointing out where I've grabbed her playfully or kicked her in my sleep or just blundered into her on some less intimate occasion. I took another long drink and just stared at Sheila and said, "Scientists Discover Life on Earth."

She kind of glanced at the floor out of the corners of her eyes and then made a little face and sighed.

"You probably don't want to hear about all this," she said.

Naturally I told her I did. So she sat there and told me all about her husband, Phil. Apparently, from what she said, he was some kind of psychopath. He had been in the Army, but had served time in prison and had finally gotten a dishonorable discharge. In spite of this, Sheila insisted he was nothing but a child, and needed a mother instead of a wife, even though he was thirty years old. Since his mother had died he was even worse than before. But of course he would be the last to realize this. He thought he was very mature and sophisticated. He played around with drugs, she said, and bragged about it like a college sophomore. He claimed the world was waking up to a new religion, the religion of the body.

But in spite of all this, he was far from being one of the flower people, because he kept a revolver in the glove compartment of his car. Sheila said she had nagged him about taking it out, until he finally said that when he did, he'd shoot her square between the tits.

That silenced her, she said. And I believed her, as much as I believed her in anything else. While she was telling me all this, about how Phil scared the hell out of her, I kept thinking of that day when I was waiting in the phone booth when she'd gone by, sitting with one cheek on his leg, snuggled up against him as he drove his new Olds.

But there was something else she had to say about him. She sat there caressing the edge of her glass with her index finger and making girl noises—like taking in her breath real quick, so that it was half sniff and half a turned-around sigh.

It was very obvious she was nervous about something else.

"This is one reason I wanted to talk to you this evening," she said. I had just refilled her glass, and by now she was acting a little drunk. Her eyes looked oily, sad and a little unfocused.

"What do *I* have to do with it?" I asked her.

She turned her glass around completely and stared at it as she did so. "Rex," she said finally, "I feel terrible about this, but I *told* him. You know. About *us*!"

"Oh, for Christ's sake!" I said. "Innocent Man Victim of Psychopath."

"Yes, I feel that way, too. I knew you'd be upset. And yet, if you knew how he was . . . I mean, he throws these absolute *tantrums,* and one night we had been arguing a lot, and . . . well, I really told him off. I didn't hold back anything, because I *wanted* to hurt him. And while I was telling him off, I mentioned your name . . . honestly, I don't know what came over me. But there it was. It was out before I knew it, and . . ."

"So what's he going to do?" I asked her.

"With him, nobody knows! There's absolutely no predicting what he'll do!"

"Swell," I said. "Just swell!"

"Please don't be mad. Above all, don't *you* get mad at me."

I told her I wouldn't, and we talked some more and drank some more. And during the course of the evening, I found out some other things. Like, she had dated a graduate student in history when she was working as a secretary for the history department in Taylor Hall, and they had a falling-out. She didn't know what it was in her that made men like her and then get so angry with her. She said she just couldn't understand it. Then she cried over the thought of this, while I sat there realizing that this thing with the graduate student explained the inscription above the urinal in Taylor Hall.

Later, we stumbled to bed, where I promptly fell asleep. But I awoke early in the morning, before it was light, and even with a great deal of co-operation failed to perform my stud duties to the eerie background music of bird songs. Then we lay there, cuddled together and breathing on each other.

She sat up and said, "Rex, I don't mind. Really. I like you anyway. Honestly. I really do."

"Hell, I'd rather not talk about it," I told her.

"But we must. There's something you don't understand about me. Or about us. Or maybe about women generally."

I looked at her. She was tapping her fingers on my shoulder and frowning at the window that was letting in enough light to show her face. She had the expression of a schoolteacher trying to explain a difficult point. I had seen Miss Temple get this look on her face many times.

"What is it that I don't understand?" I said.

"Oh, about us. You and me. I was fascinated by you the first time I heard you open your mouth. Honestly, I could just listen to you talk endlessly. Sex is important, and I certainly do love it, but it isn't everything. I mean, it isn't love. Not necessarily."

"No," I said. "Not necessarily."

She pinched my shoulder. "Oh, you don't see what I mean at all," she said. "What I mean is, there are other things, too. And as far as sex is concerned, there's always tomorrow."

"Sometimes, maybe," I said. "But not always."

She pinched my shoulder again and said, "Don't be silly. You've just been working too hard. And you still don't understand what I'm trying to say. I guess I'm just not able to express myself the way I should. But what I mean is, you have to believe in *something* in life. I believe in you. I mean, I really do. I can't explain it, but it's almost as if you were a kind of father to me. Not a *real* father, of course, but kind of what a father *ought* to be. Even your faults aren't really *awful* faults. Believe me, I'm in a position to know!"

I remained silent throughout this long speech of hers, and when she finished, I just heaved a long sigh.

"What's the matter?" she said. "Did that make you mad?"

"No," I told her. "I don't doubt but what you're telling the truth, and why should the truth make me mad?"

That explanation didn't make any kind of sense at all, but old Sheila wouldn't know the difference, bless her heart. She kept trying to find out what was wrong with me, and finally I said, "Nothing at all. The only thing is, I didn't realize I was daddy to you. Man Discovers Self Father Figure."

"Oh, it isn't like *that*!" she said. "Don't be silly!"

We went around like this for a while, trading nonexplanations for things we didn't understand ourselves, until we both got tired of it and gave it up in mutual fatigue and frustration. And on top of it all, I felt more than impotent —I felt rotten. My leg was hurting, and I was sick at my stomach and hung over all to hell and back.

By now the sun was up, and Sheila went into the bathroom and brushed her teeth with my wife's toothbrush. While she was doing this, I wondered if the act would make Sheila start speaking Spanish. Then I had fantasies about my wife coming back and, in a Mama Bear voice, asking, "Who's been using my toothbrush?"

But of course it would be long dry by then, and who would know? Or who would care?

Then I got out of bed, drank some Alka-Seltzers and told Sheila to get dressed. She said she didn't want any breakfast, so I took her back to the lot, where she got into her car and drove away. Bucky and Cripps were not there yet.

I went behind the office and just stood there beside a dark-green '67 Microbus we have had in stock for almost a year. I was sick from the booze, and I stood there about five minutes, not doing a blessed thing.

While I was standing there, I began to feel so goddam bad that I knew I would have to lie down or else pass out. For a second I considered getting in my Buick and going back home, but I wasn't sure I could make it.

So I just kind of edged over to the Microbus and climbed up in back and laid down on the back seat, with my legs doubled up.

I laid there about twenty minutes or maybe half an hour, and was almost asleep and feeling a little bit better, when I suddenly smelled cigarette smoke and heard Cripps and Bucky outside, talking. They weren't over ten or fifteen feet away, and I kept hearing Bucky kicking a tire on one of the cars. This is an irritating habit he has that used to drive Cripps half crazy, but there is no changing Bucky in something like this, so Cripps no longer says anything.

I heard Bucky say, "Do you suppose he's up at Yerby's already?"

"I wouldn't be surprised," Cripps said. "The way the big bullshitter has been drinking lately."

Bucky was silent, but I could almost see him nodding his face up and down inside his fat neck, with that toothpick in his mouth.

"One thing sure," Bucky said, a few seconds later, "he hasn't gone too far without his Buick."

"One of these days, we're going to read about the son of a bitch dropping over dead with a heart attack," Cripps said.

"What do you suppose will happen to the lot?" Bucky asked.

"Hell, his wife would sell it in a minute."

"I know that. But who to?"

"Who knows?"

"Shee-yut," Bucky said after a few seconds. "It wouldn't make no difference to me. I'm sick and tired of the son of a bitch anyway."

"Rex?"

"Well, him, too. But I was thinking of the lot."

"I just wonder how much fucking money he *is* making

off of this place. I just wonder how many sales he steals right out from under us. You *know* he's always screwing around with the account. Him and his big bullshit mouth! He thinks he can buy us off with coffee and cigarettes, after hogging all the sales! The bastard doesn't think we even suspect. I just wonder how much he robs us of!"

"With him," Bucky said, "you never can tell. When's the last time he's said *anything* you can believe?"

"Well, he'll get it someday. I mean, you don't live the way that old bastard lives and get away with it."

"That's the truth," Bucky said. He was quiet a couple seconds; then his voice changed a little, and he said, "I'm going down and check that blue Pontiac out. Tell him where I am if he comes back."

"He probably won't even know you're missing," Cripps said.

Then they walked off, and I laid there another ten minutes or so before I climbed out the door opposite the office. Nobody saw me get out, and I circled a couple cars and approached the office from the direction of Yerby's.

When Cripps saw me, he was smoking a Marlboro, and he said, "Bucky's checking out that Pontiac, Rex."

I nodded and said that was fine. I couldn't look Cripps in the face after what I'd just heard. I went into the office and tried to work on some papers, but I couldn't do it, and after a few minutes I was just sitting there with my head in my hands. I was so sick and sad and tired, I couldn't move. Bucky hadn't returned with the Pontiac yet, and Cripps was nowhere in sight. Rick Ruggles and Willie Byrd were busy at work over in the filling station. There was nobody around, and I was glad of it, because I don't think I was up to talking to anybody.

After a few minutes, Cripps came in the office and grabbed a few more Marlboros from the cup and stuck one in his mouth. "What's the matter?" he said. "Not up to par this morning, Rex?"

I just looked at him for an instant. In both eyes, the one that saw and the one that was always looking somewhere else.

"Maybe you ought to get a hair of the dog that bit you," he said. He lit the Marlboro with his Zippo, and then clapped the lighter shut. "Might be good for what ails you, Rex."

I still couldn't answer him, but he didn't seem to notice. He just took a couple drags on his cigarette and stared out at my cars.

Then a man came up into the lot, looking over the line of VW's, and Cripps went out to wait on him.

Who would have believed it of old Cripps? And of old Bucky? I had loved those two boys like sons. I thought of them dancing in their hillbilly outfits the night before, and I just couldn't stand it any more, so I went out in back of the office, where nobody could see how goddam bad I felt.

21

But I bounced back pretty well, partly because of business. We weren't able to match that first day, but the week was really turning out to be a good one. There was a fine crowd every night through Wednesday, and we made tremendous sales. On Thursday, I agreed with Gunther to keep the Hatfield Four on an extra week. There was a lot of juice to be milked out of this big fat Holstein baby, yet.

Also on Thursday, I got a phone call from Homer Winslow, and he told me that he would like me to look over the film he'd made and sign a model release on it if it was okay. I asked him how soon, and he said that very afternoon if I could make it.

That was fine, because I wanted to get back to the lot right after dinner. There are a thousand things that can come up with an organization like ours, particularly if there is the Hatfield Four (including Little Hermie, who I once said to Gunther made it more like the Hatfield Three and a Half) entertaining. The problems that come bubbling to the surface can give you nightmares if you think of those two goddam boys of mine, Bucky and Cripps, having to handle them. Especially after what I had overheard them saying.

Anyhow, Winslow told me to come about four o'clock; so I went over to Taylor Hall, after a quick one at Yerby's, and there was the professor, waiting for me in his office. He was reading from a thick sheaf of yellow papers. He was sitting there in his swivel chair, with his glasses pulled up on his forehead like the hairiest old-fashioned aviator in history, and frowning.

When he saw me, he waved his hand, and I said, "Scientists Say Bees Give Honey," and then we went down to another room, where the black blinds were already closed and there was a projector standing on a table.

"I got things ready for you so you wouldn't have to wait," he said, squatting down with two loud knee cracks and plugging the projector cord into a floor socket.

I told him that was fine, and started to say something else—just to pass the time of day—but Winslow had the projector going right away.

As the first scratches appeared on the screen, he said, "Of course, you probably know they think I'm crazy about all this. Some professor from a college in the boondocks."

"They do?" I said.

"Yes. But maybe this film will help convince them. I haven't been able to diagram from the film yet. That's the important part. Nobody seems to understand how I'm going to establish my co-ordinates. This is just the raw material, although it will be shown along with the diagrams. What I'm saying is, the release you sign won't apply to anything on which your image appears other than the film you're watching now."

"Professor, Car King Reach Agreement," I said.

On the screen there were several panning shots of the lot, with the sounds of traffic on the street. It picked up the sound real well. And at one place I even heard Bucky call out Cripps's name, although neither of them could be seen at the moment. It was very strange, because it was in black and white, and it looked a little like a documentary or news report on television, because I don't have color TV yet. No music, of course. Just the clicking of the projector and the black and white.

Then a man was approaching the camera. I recognized him as a young fellow named Chambers, who is just starting out in insurance with his dad. I remembered selling him a nice clean TR5 one morning.

Anyway, young Chambers came forward, and then I see my shoulder come into view as I am turning around, saying something inaudible to somebody (probably Bucky or Cripps) in the background. And then I turn around and am shaking hands with this Chambers lad.

Christ, what a shock! I've heard my wife say a thousand times that the camera adds ten pounds to a person's appearance, by which she means a woman's appearance. This is one of her favorite conversational facts. And since I weigh over twice what the average female movie star weighs, I suppose I look at least twenty pounds heavier.

But God Almighty, was that gimpy, dark-faced, thick-bodied old sinner *myself?* He limped up to young

Chambers and shook his hand and growled, "Chambers, right?"

And Chambers, faced with this wicked old bastard in the string tie, understandably hesitated and kind of gulped before he shook hands. He would probably count his fingers later, and who could blame him?

Then I was in action. I never realized how hoarse my voice is. Probably from whiskey and cigars. I had never realized how I would sing and chant when I got wound up. I mean, I *realized* it, but goddam if I realized it was exactly like this.

And thick in the body? Sweet Jesus, I almost looked like Randall.

Naturally, however, the shock began to wear off. You can get used to anything. And every now and then, after a while, I would chuckle at an argument I heard myself use, or at the way I would twist something around.

Christ, I was quick at thinking on my feet! This, I realized then, was part of my charisma. Not just the logic alone, but the spirit, the confidence behind the logic.

And, by God, when I would wind up and start punching the index finger of one hand into the palm of the other, people would just come unglued before your eyes. My charisma would almost go out of control at such times, so that you'd think it might even break the lens of the camera, the way they say Caruso's high C would break a water glass.

When the film was finished, I was sitting there sweating like a horse, for some reason, and I wanted to get out of that dark room into the daylight. The only dark room I felt like being in was a bar, and that was exactly where I intended to go.

Winslow explained the model release to me, and showed me how the film was identified and how this was expressed on the release.

I held the pen for a couple seconds, almost wishing I

didn't have to sign. It was too goddam much, even if it was flattering in a way. I mean, not many people have anything special about them, let alone charisma.

But I signed, saying, "Man Finds Judge, Self Guilty."

After I'd signed the release, Winslow patted my shoulder and said, "Did it look like the real McCoy up there on the screen?"

Then he surprised me by suggesting that we have a drink. "Do you have time before you get back to the lot?" he asked.

I told him I did, and we went out of Taylor Hall and walked a block and a half to a bar called the Beech Grove, which is a name I have always liked, although I never figured out what it meant; the present owner doesn't know, either.

Inside, Winslow ordered Jack Daniel's bourbon for both of us, which also surprised me, because I thought maybe he would be drinking wine.

We sat there and drank a couple and talked.

Winslow did most of the talking, naturally, and it occurred to me once more that for a man who was so impressed by my charisma, this jasper did very little listening and a hell of a lot of talking. But I didn't mind particularly, because when I talk, I like to sell something. Other times, I don't mind letting other people talk as much as they like. They can settle the world problems and the race problems and all that. I want to sell a two-and-a-half-thousand-dollar car or keep my mouth shut.

Winslow said, "One thing that really intrigues me about all this is you possess all the expansive virtues, which are becoming more and more outmoded. Rex, you are an atavism."

He went on to say that the powers of personal charisma would someday, in his way of thinking, be totally outmoded, because charisma was usually used to trick or cheat people, to make them believe something that wasn't true. Like selling Metzger a dog of a '66 Buick and making him think it was just great.

"No sir," he said. "Someday, things will be run by computers. And do you know what you are?"

I shook my head no.

"You are an old-time Mississippi riverboat gambler. Deep down, that's exactly what you are."

The way he said it, I realized right then that old Homer Winslow kind of admired me for this. And as a matter of fact, I kind of liked it myself.

I was surprised at the change in this bird. He seemed downright mellow, as if he had just gone through something that few men are given to experience. His hair and sideburns and mustache were wilder than I had ever seen them, but his eyes were sort of faraway and misty.

Of course, it could have been the Jack Daniel's. But there was something else there, too. I guess the word is "contrite." The wild-ass old critic of small-town America had given way to this indulgent little creature lighting his pipe, methodically turning it upside down and puffing away in a mild and philosophic mood.

"I've been going through a lot lately," he said.

"That so?"

"Yes. I won't bore you with the details, but I just want you to realize that I know how shitty I've been the past month or so. When a man's unhappy inside, he projects. You know what I mean?"

"Sure."

Then he started talking about this thing he'd been going through, and how it was like a religious experience, in some ways. And how it was all connected with charisma.

"Charisma is a projection of one's life style," he said.

"The stronger and more vital and more vivid the life style, the more a man is prompted to express it in the total rhetoric available to him. This composite rhetoric, when it is intensified and focused the way it is in your behavior, becomes charisma."

"We're all kind of public-relations men for our beliefs, then," I said.

Winslow gazed at me a moment, and then nodded. "That's just about the way it is," he said.

Then I entered into the spirit of the thing, so that before long we were lamenting the end of individuality. Because charisma is a very personal thing. As Winslow pointed out, it *originates* in personality. All of it. He called it "an expression of general power emanating from a unique source." He repeated this formula several times in his conversation.

By the time Winslow had to leave, I was hungry. So I sat there in the Beech Grove and had a sirloin and salad, and three or four cups of coffee. I finished in reasonably good shape, looked at my watch and saw that it was only fifteen minutes until the Hatfield Four would show up. I got a quick idea for a sign on my desk, and I wrote it down in my little notebook: "A sale (boat) a day keeps the dock away. Stay afloat financially."

Of course, I meant dry dock.

I got in my Buick and drove to the lot, where there were three phone numbers listed for me. One of them was Sheila's, so I called that one first, and she told me that she was out of touch with her husband. He had moved somewhere else, probably went to a motel under an assumed name, and she hadn't heard from him for two days now.

I told her to relax, but she said that wasn't all; that she had seen him following her that morning in his new Olds, which he had taken back from her. He followed her to work.

"He doesn't know where you live," she said, "but he knows your name, of course."

"You mean he's looking for me?" I asked her.

"He might be," she said. "You might keep your eye out for him, because he might be following you around in his car. Oh, I forgot."

"Forgot what?"

"Well, I guess maybe you knew. He brought me to your lot that evening. So he knows what you look like, because he saw you up there on the stand, talking through the microphone."

"Well, I can't worry about that," I said. "And you shouldn't, either."

"But you just don't understand how *violent* he is, and *unstable.*"

"You'll be all right."

"But I wonder if I shouldn't call the police."

"No. Just sit tight. There's a lot more bullshit in this world than there is bulls." The grammar of that got kind of fouled up, but I thought it sounded pretty good anyway.

"I wish we were together," she said. "I feel safe when I'm around you, somehow."

"Sure. You're always safe with Daddy. Labor, Management Agree on Price Hike."

She was quiet a minute after I said that, but then she said, "I didn't mean that the way it sounded the other night. Honestly, Rex. You've got to believe me!"

I didn't know how else she *could* have meant it, but I told her it was all right. Then Cripps came up with a question about a credit report, so I told Sheila I had to hang up. And I told her once more that everything was going to be all right. The truth was, I had already forgotten about this creep husband of hers by the time I saw Merle and Gunther come on the lot, talking together. That is, Gunther was talking and Merle was silent, as usual.

I spent quite a bit of time that evening with Gunther. Partly because things were getting to be pretty slow on the lot, for the first time in the present campaign, but also because I was beginning to kind of like the old dog. One thing about Gunther: he had never lost his spirit. You could look at his face, which was as cracked as the crater of a volcano, and you could tell the old son of a bitch had been through a hell of a lot. But he still came up fighting. That is what I would call character.

Anyway, we stood together and talked quite a bit that evening. Didn't say much worth reporting. He was wearing his string tie, as usual, and I was wearing mine, as usual. We both stood casually, side by side, smoking cigars and using a great deal of blasphemous and obscene and comforting language. Every now and then, one of us would lean forward a little and spit a heavy gob between our feet.

Up there on the brightly lighted bandstand, the Hatfield Four were raising the usual happy hell. I let Bucky and Cripps take care of most of the sales, because they had both fallen behind, relatively, and needed all they could get. I figured I shouldn't be too hard on them for what they'd said the other day. Not only that, where would they go if I fired them? And who'd I get to replace their screwball asses?

Local Dealer Believes in Giving Bastards Break.

Little Hermie cried out that he didn't want to be left all alone, but he didn't seem to be quite as forlorn as he had been earlier. Maybe he didn't feel very good this evening. Also, the Hatfield Four didn't seem to be quite as good as they were at first. I would guess I had heard most of their repertoire six or seven times by now, and the novelty had worn off. It was still enjoyable, but not as much of a sensation. Maybe the public felt this way, too, and that was why they weren't crowding the lot the way they had those first few days.

People can get used to anything, as I said before, and that is both an encouraging and a sad truth. Maybe charisma lasts longer than other things.

I suppose if I had watched Winslow's film long enough, I could reconcile myself to being that ugly, whiskey-voiced, spraddle-assed old son of a bitch on the screen.

God knows who would see that man going through his routines on the movie screen.

Would it be possible that my charisma would work on them, too? On the charisma experts studying my voice inflections and gesticulations? Or would they, like Homer Winslow, appear to be immune to the power they were studying?

Later on that evening, Gunther and I went to Yerby's and had a couple. Yerby recited several verses of "Dangerous Dan McGrew," which he only does about every month, when he has a skinful.

Gunther thought it was great.

I paid for the drinks and went home, where I didn't feel a damn bit good.

22

In any account like this, there are a lot of things that have to be left out. For example, I haven't been mentioning the buying trips I have to make to keep the freshest cars in the state on my lot, or the Rotary meetings, which I always go to. Or having drinks and cards and dinner with the Dwight Klepingers one evening. Klepinger is worth at least a couple million dollars, and is one of the local barons whose money came originally from corn and hogs. My wife would appreciate this, since she is a snob and thinks I don't put enough emphasis on money and social position.

I guess it's no secret by now that I love to trade, as well as buy and sell. That is, wheel and deal a little. For instance, when the college tore down Chatham Hall a couple years ago, I got in touch with the contractor (a man named Blivens—a colored man, brother to the man I sold a red '70 VW to recently) and bought every blessed brick out of Chatham Hall. I now have those bricks stacked in a triple lot I own on the west side of town. Not too far from Randall's house. You can never tell when they will come in handy. They are fine old bricks, hard as fieldstone and a hundred years old, at least, and they will make three or four fine little houses or a dozen real fancy patios one of these days.

I also took in a quarter horse once on a station wagon. I still board that goddam horse, which has the silly-ass name of Skylark, with a farmer named McKinstry. He has only one eye. (McKinstry does.) He also raises Scotch pines for Christmas trees.

And on one of these days—I forget which—I called Ted Bascom, the county engineer, and asked about straightening out a road near town, which is a real bottleneck and traffic hazard. I am always up to something, as my wife is always up to telling me.

And then there were a couple mornings of golf, which I always play in the nineties whether I work hard at it or don't give a damn.

So there were other things happening these days, even with the Hatfield Four sales campaign going strong.

The morning after I had seen the film, I took my time getting up and about. I shaved about nine-thirty and doused my face in English Leather, which my wife says I use too much of.

The mail came, and there wasn't anything except a bill from the dry cleaner and a little magazine in a brown wrapper.

I opened the magazine up, because I didn't remember subscribing to it, and saw it was titled *The Rumbling Red Wheelbarrow,* which seemed like a hell of a name for a magazine.

I opened it up, and the first thing I see is this poem (at least it was scattered all over the page like one of those modernistic poems), with the words "fuck" and "shit" in it. Then it was I had this suspicion, and when I turned to the table of contents, sure enough, there was the name Philip McCoy alongside a poem called "Paternities." Page 25.

So I turned to page 25, and here is what I read:

PATERNITIES

by Philip McCoy

Child, let us finally ask:
"Who indeed is your father,
and where?" Child,
you will long ask this question.
Will long, listen for his voice.

Let me bear witness to you,
and tell you how it is with me
(Do you think any truth,
Walt Whitman,
is irrelevant between us?):

My father is most stupendously strong
where he is ignorant.
My father is beautiful precisely
where he cannot understand what,
what I am about. My father
knows
does not know.

My father does not go gentle
Hell, no,
will not go!
but is a gentleman in spite of all.
Does not ask others.
Does not make excuses.
He does not pity himself
or anyone else.
He does not want to understand,
but will listen any way.

Although his world seems simpler,
the truth is that he himself
is partly responsible for this fact.
He is simply a simple, simple man
in a changing, changing time.
He is a hero with words and deeds,
but is vulnerable in more than heel.

My father is a wrong-headed man
(which is to say an honest one).
Part of what he was meant to become
is me. He is therefore
this division, and this pain.
My father will not read these words,
Child.
Forgive.
Remember.

I mused upon this poem for a while. Was it really about me, Regius McCoy, that Phil had written? Or was it about some symbolic father or just any father?

I didn't think it was much of a poem, and I didn't know why he had written it like that, but there was something interesting about it, because it was written by my boy. The one I had tried to get interested in hunting and fishing, but nothing doing beyond the age of twelve or thirteen. The one who had made up his mind very early to be as quiet and withdrawn (a little like Randall) as his father was loud and outgoing.

I read the thing again, and wondered if he had sent it home just for his mother to read, or whether he had secretly wanted me to read it . . . especially that part about "my father will not read these words."

Or did this part mean that his real father (spiritual father or something like that) was not me at all, and therefore, even if I did read it, in some deeper sense the lines would still be true?

This thinking brought me back to one of the oldest jokes in my life: Was I the real McCoy? Or, who *is* the real McCoy? If, as the poem says, Phil is part of me, is *he* the real McCoy then? Who is the real *anything*, for Christ's sake?

You can see that this line of questioning wouldn't do anything to the price of peaches, so I finally threw *The Rumbling Red Wheelbarrow* on the sofa and went out to my Buick. Then I drove down to Gestler's Lunch and ordered breakfast, spelling out every single thing I wanted, as usual, to Sally, the world's dumbest goddam waitress.

23

As I sat there waiting to be served, I looked through the window at the people walking up and down the sidewalks. And then, on the other side of the street, who should I see but my brother, Randall. He was all dressed up, ambling along like a riverboat going upstream, without looking to left or right, and he turned into T. F. Hanaway's office.

Undoubtedly, he was visiting Hanaway for another codicil having to do with a laundry ticket once used by Ambrose Bierce, or maybe a letter by Mark Twain or something.

But as I continued to stare out the window, I saw something that made me come awake a little bit more. This was a brand-new Olds convertible, with the top up, parked on my side of the street. Inside was a tanned, bearded fellow looking at the entrance to T. F.'s office, just as I had been doing a couple seconds before.

Only, as I looked at him, I realized he might not be exactly tanned; he looked like he was a Puerto Rican or maybe a very light-skinned Negro. I was almost certain he wasn't all white. I think it was the eyes and the cheekbones more than the lips or nose. But there it was. And when I'd gotten a glimpse of him before, I hadn't even seen enough of his face to notice the little mustache and goatee.

A lot of things flew through my mind at that moment. But most of all, I kept hearing that corny joke going through my mind: "Hello deh. Ah is yoh new NEIGH-buh!"

Right then Sally served me my eggs and hash, and I sat there eating them while I continued watching Sheila's crazy husband watching the entrance that Randall, my crazy brother, had just gone in.

When I finished breakfast, this jasper hadn't moved. He was still sitting there waiting, so I didn't bother to light up a D. M. panetela. Instead, I went out back through the kitchen, which surprised the two old women working there, and went two lots up to where my own car was parked, and got in.

Then I drove back onto the street about a hundred yards behind the Oldsmobile and waited. Eventually, a woman pulled out of a parking place, so I took it.

Up ahead of me, I could still see Sheila's husband, Phil, waiting in his new Olds. And I could still see that Randall hadn't come out yet.

It was obvious to me by now that Phil thought fat, crazy Randall was me. There was no other connection, and the thought kind of shocked me.

About ten minutes later, Randall emerged from the doorway of the building and ambled back up the street towards his pickup truck. There was a parking ticket on the windshield, and old Randall stopped and stared at it for what seemed like another ten minutes, trying to figure out what it was.

Then it dawned on him, and he took the envelope-ticket out from under the windshield wiper, read the instructions carefully and put two quarters inside. Then he moved up the street to one of the meters with a box on it for paying the fine and dropped the ticket in.

All this time, Sheila's husband was watching him intently. His head didn't waver from its focus on my fat and eccentric brother. And when Randall finally got in his truck, Phil started his car; and of course I started mine.

Then Randall drove away, Sheila's husband in pursuit of him, and me in pursuit of Sheila's husband. The three of us drove through the center of town, and I was soon aware that Randall was simply returning home. As usual, he didn't exceed thirty-five miles per hour, even on the wide stretch of highway that connects his street with the main part of town.

When he approached his house, Randall slowed down and eased his truck into the driveway. By this time, Sheila's husband was practically on top of him, and I was only thirty or forty yards in the rear.

I could feel the old sensation that meant I might have to get out of the car and go into some sort of action if this man decided to confront Randall. It was like the old days in the Marines.

But nothing happened. After he had slowed down, Phil suddenly gunned his engine and sent that new Olds of his up to fifty in about three seconds, and then screeched his tires going around a corner, where he disappeared.

I didn't follow him. I just coasted up the street, wiping the sweat off my face with a handkerchief, and then after a bit I drove slowly and sedately back to the lot. Apparently, everything was going to be all right, for a while at least.

But something had to be done about the crazy bastard, I could see that. First of all, he shouldn't be allowed to go on thinking that Randall was me.

What I would try to do would be to have some kind of talk with Phil and let him know who I was.

I kept joking with myself and saying that I was the real McCoy, no matter what this episode with Randall suggested, and no matter what Homer Winslow's film made me look like.

I suddenly felt something like warmth and affection for old Randall; seeing him so fat and incompetent and absent-minded as he ambled out of T. F. Hanaway's office made me want to help him. Brace him up and give the poor old son of a bitch another chance.

The more I thought of these things, the more it occurred to me that in this whole screwed-up business, there was no one any crazier than myself.

Human Identities Uncertain, Scientists Say.

Whoever and whatever the real McCoy was, there didn't seem to be any precise time when I myself could look at him and recognize him for what he really was.

Later on that evening, I had two of those different spells I have mentioned. The first was during a lull in business, along about ten o'clock, when I was sitting in my office alone. Hermie gave his little lonesome cry, and for some reason I started laughing to myself. And then I really broke up, laughing out loud with all the stops out, like an idiot. It occurred to me that if Bucky and Cripps saw me, they would think I'd lost my mind.

Madman Makes Money Despite Madness.

As a matter of fact, Bucky did come in a few minutes later, when I had calmed down a little. He settled one of his big, bushel-sized cheeks on the edge of the desk and said, "Well, how's it going?"

We chatted a few minutes, and then, for some reason, I said, "Bucky, tell me about yourself."

Bucky stood up like somebody had given him an electric shock with a cattle prod. He took a gigantic tug at his crotch and said, "Shee-yut!" and went back outside to mingle with the crowd.

Then I was kind of sorry I had teased him like that. So I busied myself with some paperwork for a while, and then about twenty minutes or a half hour later I had this other kind of spell, where everything turned kind of unreal and got far away, as it had in Altizer's Department Store.

So help me, the lighted bandstand didn't look any closer than the Shell sign a half-mile down the street, or a fat star. It was like all my vision was suddenly crowded up into the space of a keyhole, like those wide-lens photographs you see.

Well, I came out of it all right. Sweating as usual, and shaky as hell. I just kind of sat in the office and waited until things got all right. Which they did.

24

The next afternoon, I was sitting in my office doing some paperwork when I glanced out on the lot, and there was Gunther coming toward me.

He came into the office and said, "McCoy, how's about your self and my self settling down and having a drink?"

I suppose it was inevitable that the two of us should get

together, and after I'd cleaned myself up a little and loaded Gunther into my Buick, it seemed the most natural thing in the world for us to head for Yerby's.

Well, we sat there and had a couple, talking old men's talk and stopping every now and then to cough or maybe go take a leak.

Finally Gunther said, "Do you know what I haven't drank in a long, long time?"

"What?" I asked him.

"Corn whiskey. I mean, homemade cornsqueezings. Stumphole whiskey, white lightning. Moonshine. Mule kick. Whatever you might wish to call it."

"I haven't, either," I told him.

"But he didn't seem to hear me. He went on, musing and looking sentimental out of his sad wet eyes. "No siree, I haven't drank any of that stuff for a long, long, *long* time."

"You act as if you miss it," I said.

That seemed to astonish him. "*Miss* it," he said, sinking a look about three inches behind my eyes. "Why, I should sure as hell say I *do* miss it! When it's made right, that there is delicious stuff."

"Some people like it, I guess," I told him.

"And when the roll is called up yonder," Gunther said, reverently shaking his head back and forth, "I'm one of them." Then he leaned closer to me to whisper, but his voice was still about the loudest thing going in Yerby's: "I don't suppose this place carries it under the bar, do they?"

"No. Yerby wouldn't have it. But I do know a place about eight miles out of town where you can get it."

"Are you telling me true?" Gunther said, leaning back in his chair like a cardinal who's just witnessed a miracle.

"Sure."

"Well, tell me how to get there, will you?"

I looked at my watch and said, "Hell, I'll just take you there myself."

"You don't have to do that," Gunther said.

"No sense putting it off," I said, standing up. "Delay Connected with Mental Illness. Come on. I want to give it a try myself. It's been years since I've tasted that stuff. But I know old Liggett will have some."

"Is that his name, Liggett?" Gunther said. And I told him it was, and explained to him that old Liggett was a master of the craft . . . a Guinea, which is to say, a man with Negro, white and Creek Indian blood in his veins.

We went out to my car, which had a traffic ticket. I put two quarters in the envelope and stuck the whole business in the little yellow box they keep for them. And of course this made me think of Randall getting a ticket the day before, and that made me remind myself to tip him off about Sheila's husband. Or at least do *something* about the whole stupid situation.

But I figured that could wait. We got in the car, and Gunther, who had this obnoxious habit of repeating things he'd just said, over and over, said, "Yes sir, I haven't drank any good old-fashioned corn whiskey for a long, long, *long* time!"

"I know it," I said. "You've already told me that."

But of course he wasn't put off by my tone. He simply sat there like the king of the cats, smoking his cigar and flicking ashes all over his fat abdomen and my car upholstery. God, he was sloppier than I am.

I was a little surprised, because the drinks had really gone to my head, and I was having trouble keeping the car straight on the road.

We went out of town in the direction of Wingback Lake but then turned off on this gravel county road, which winds through the hills until it comes to Ernie Liggett's little shingle house.

But we didn't make it to Ernie's house, because as I was going around a sharp turn on a steep downgrade, my car skidded in the gravel, smacked head on into another car that must have been coming just as fast, and we skidded over the edge of the road into a twenty-foot gulley.

Like anything of this sort, it happened so quick I didn't really have a chance to find out what had taken place. The impact of my Buick against a tree at the bottom of the gulley knocked me cold as a goddam frozen fish. I figured I was doing about thirty or thirty-five—which was too fast on a road like that. I was also a little bit drunk, which didn't help.

I don't know how fast the other car was going.

Briefly and hazily, I regained consciousness in the emergency room of the hospital, and then they immediately put me to sleep again. My head felt like somebody had hammered a whole keg of sixpenny nails in it, and I bubbled when I breathed. I felt like I was living inside a dirty lake.

The next time I came to, I hurt all over—more than I had before, because now I was completely conscious.

There was no one about, but after a while a nurse came by and said, "Well, you've come to." That's all she said, and she didn't smile or anything.

Later on, a couple of doctors came by, and a different nurse was with them. They didn't seem very cheery, either. They just shined a little light in my eyes and looked me all over and prodded me here and there. Then they told me I would recover all right.

Finally I asked them how Gunther was, and one of them answered, "Not so bad."

"I wish we could say as much for the girl in the other car," the other one said.

"What about her?" I asked.

"It's hard to tell whether she'll make it or not."

"Who is it?"

"Her name's Patti Nieder. She's a student at the college."

25

Everybody was polite to me, I'll have to admit that. But I was feeling bad, all the same. Gunther was recovering pretty well. He had a concussion, a badly bruised hip, a broken kneecap and a lot of cuts. The head injuries weren't bad, though. He was in a ward up the hall.

I pieced together the information that I had gotten a bad concussion, fractures of the left arm, nose and four ribs. Along with some deep cuts about the face and a dislocated shoulder. It must have been a hell of a jolt, and in those circumstances you can't tell what is going to have to give.

Patti Nieder was still on the critical list, I heard. The worst thing about her was a broken back, for God's sake. Even if she lived, they figured she might be paralyzed for the rest of her life.

The third day, I had visitors, although I was still pretty groggy and my vision was blurred. The first was Cripps, who depressed me all to hell. He just sat there, as far as I could tell, and looked at the goddam wall with one eye and in the direction of Chillicothe with the other. He didn't know what to say, and when I tried to ask him something about the lot, he'd just sigh and give pessimistic answers.

Then Bucky came by for a while, after Cripps left, and talked about Cincinnati's chances for the pennant this year, which were not as good as Bucky would have made them if he were God. When he was about to leave, who should walk in but Betty, bringing me a bouquet of red roses, a pint of Jack Daniel's, Green Label, and a message from Randall to keep my chin up.

She smuggled the booze to me, but I was still too sore and blurred and groggy to hide it, and a nurse found it about ten minutes after Betty left, and confiscated it without saying a word.

When I asked the nurse about Patti Nieder, she said, "That's the third time you've asked me today. She's just the same."

Then she walked out.

About twenty minutes after that, Winslow came in. Naturally, I had trouble getting him in focus, too, but I could see that he'd gotten a haircut and tamed his sideburns considerably and shaved his mustache off. Also, the bastard was wearing a string tie. So help me. He sat there at the foot of the bed talking to me like I was about to face the electric chair or something.

While he was talking, I vowed that I wouldn't ask about Patti Nieder any more. What is done is done, I kept telling myself. And the only clean and decent thing to do is to keep on going. I have known too many people in this world who feel guilty about things, and believe me, they are dirty. Their own guilt makes them dirty. *Every*body suffers if you feel guilty. It's a self-indulgence, and it's sick.

Naturally, Winslow was feeling guilty or disturbed about something. After a bit, I could smell bourbon on the poor son of a bitch's breath. He was sitting there, drunk as half a goddam skunk, rubbing his hand all over his face and sighing.

After he'd asked all about the accident and Patti Nieder, he fell silent a while, and then he said, "Rex, have you heard?"

"Heard what?"

"Obviously you haven't," he muttered. Then he lighted a cigar, in spite of the no-smoking signs all around. He dropped the match on the floor and leaned over towards me. "Nobody understands," he said. "They don't know what we've done."

"What *have* we done? You mean the charisma thing?"

"Yes. They think it's all obvious, or else they think it's invalid. They don't *really* see what it is I'm trying to show; but they think they do, and they just think I'm some crackpot from Boondocks College in Nowheresville."

I told him that was too bad, but there was something else he wanted to say. And after he sat there puffing on the cigar a few finutes, he gave me a real deep look and said, "Rex, do you know something?"

"No," I said. "What?"

"I think the sons of bitches are right. For all the wrong reasons, but, goddammit, they're right."

"What do you mean?"

"I mean, I've gone over our film about a hundred times, and I've charted every goddam thing you've done—every raised eyebrow, every punch of the index finger into the other hand, every pat on the shoulder, every voice inflection . . . and, in addition, every rhetorical device known to the ancient sophists, and a few you've invented yourself, and . . . and it is gone."

"The charisma?"

"The charisma. Fled. Evaporated." He held the cigar up before him like a test tube. "Gone up like smoke."

"Which means it can't be measured after all, I suppose."

"That's the obvious conclusion. But these bastards are hooked on being scientists, and there's something in them that rebels at such a possibility . . . still, there it is. I've measured everything there was. I've established indices, terminals, guide points . . . and I've quantified everything, including the decibels of your friendly clincher, which I'll never forget. How does it go? 'Let's just go over to that desk over there and make this baby officially yours!' "

He shook his head at the thought of it.

I wasn't thinking too straight, because I was half high on painkillers, and I said, "So there's no such thing as charisma; is that it?"

Winslow stood up then and said, "Will you, for Christ's sweet sake, open your eyes and look at me? Do you think I don't know what I'm doing, for God's sake? Do you? Look here: string tie, Dutch Masters panetela cigar. I've had a half-pint of Jack Daniel's since lunchtime, and my stomach can't even *take* the stuff! Oh, it's ridiculous. Utterly ridiculous, and when I get a good look at myself I could die laughing. What else do you want?"

I looked at him and saw that it was true—all of it. I took a long sigh and kind of shook my head as much as the bandages and pain would allow.

"Do you know something?" he said. "I think I would make a pretty good salesman, if I wanted to give it a try."

"Come give it a try," I said.

"No. No. You don't understand. This is just something I've got to go through. Like measles for a goddam kid."

"Yes, I guess selling cars would kind of louse up your social ideals."

"Bullshit," Winslow said. "You horse's ass, you've corrupted me clear down to my convictions."

"Sounds like I have," I said.

Who would have thought I had been getting through to the bastard? I didn't feel good at all; this was a sad thing to contemplate. Whatever charisma is, the one who has it can't predict how it will work on others.

"Hell," he said a minute later. "I don't even know what I'm saying. I'm stale on teaching. It's a pain in the ass when you come right down to it. But I'd probably feel the same about selling a bunch of goddam beaten-down cars."

I told him our stock wasn't beaten down, and he ought to take a better look the next time he was out there on the lot.

He shook his head and said, "I know what it is: conviction. That's what you've got. Most people who have as much conviction as you do are goddam fools, but somehow you just *miss* being a fool. And that makes all the difference, I guess."

I didn't particularly like that interpretation, and I kind of growled at him out of my bandages.

But Winslow ignored that and said, "The thing that haunts me, Rex, is that your charisma operates on people . . . and lays them out like bowling pins, and they don't even know what's happening. The thing that bothers me is that *you're the world champion, and nobody in the whole fucking world except me knows it.* I've studied these effects in every possible dimension for fifteen years, and believe me, nobody can come close to you. Except for the accident of history, you could have been . . . I don't know what you could have been."

I thought of some lines from the "Country Churchyard" Miss Temple had made us learn:

> Full many a gem of purest ray serene
> The dark unfathom'd caves of ocean bear:
> Full many a flower is born to blush unseen,
> And waste its sweetness on the desert air.

Homer Winslow was saying *I* was a flower, blushing unseen, and wasting my sweetness on farmers and small-town yokels the likes of Bucky and Cripps.

I remembered when I was in school and called upon to recite these lines, I had pronounced it "dessert" and the class broke up. I think Miss Temple must have hated me; I was her nemesis. Maybe our two charismas were in conflict, even then; I had never considered it this way.

"What are you thinking about? You feeling worse?"

I shook my head no. "I'm all right. I was just thinking about what you said. Boondocks Salesman Found Charismatic."

He nodded and puffed on his cigar. Just then a nurse came by and scolded him for smoking, took the cigar away and thumped down the hallway.

Winslow stood up. "Well," he said, "I've got to follow the Dutch Masters cigar."

We shook hands and said good-by. Before he left, he said, "Style—that's what you've got. You know what I mean? Life style. Don't ever let the shifty bastards talk you out of it!"

After he left, I dozed off for a while, and then I woke up again and started thinking a thousand thoughts, and wishing a nurse or attendant would come by so I could ask about the girl again. Then, as quick as I would think it, I would vow I wouldn't give them a chance to see me crawl, and I wouldn't ask them a goddam thing.

Accident Victim Rejects Guilt.

By the time these thoughts were settling down, I had what I at first thought was a hallucination. I looked up, and standing there in the doorway was Clendon Metzger in a bathrobe. He was staring at me wide-eyed and not saying a word.

"I wondered if you were asleep," he said, when I kind of nodded.

"No, I'm not," I said.

"I see you're not. I came here for my hernia operation. I told you about it. Remember?"

I told him I remembered; and then I asked how Mother

was, and he said all right. Also, he said the hernia operation had been successful.

Then he just stood there without saying anything for a few seconds, until he finally took a breath and said, "The Buick's holding up just fine."

Then he walked away without asking how I was doing at all.

26

When visiting hours came around the next day, Betty came by, bringing the mail from the house. It was all bills and circulars except for a picture postcard from my wife addressed to me. It showed some big cathedral in living color, and of course the card was written in Spanish.

Betty told me she had wired my wife right after my accident, and then on the next day, but hadn't gotten any answer. "I think she may be on a special tour of some kind," Betty said.

I told her that was possible. Then I lifted the postcard up to her and said, "Can you read Spanish?"

Betty said, "No. Can't you?"

I shook my head no, and Betty said, "Well, why does she write to you in Spanish if you can't read it?"

"Who knows?" I said.

"I'm sure she'll come back soon," Betty told me. "I'm going to send her another wire today."

I thought about that for a while, and then I asked her what old Randall was doing, and she surprised me by saying he was writing his memoirs.

"His *what?*" I asked her.

But she repeated what she'd said, sounding like it was the most natural thing in the world for my 280-pound brother to write his memoirs.

For God's sake, wasn't there any humility left *anywhere* in the world? What had Randall ever done that anybody would want to read about his life? Could you imagine reading about this son of a bitch going back to his railroad cars every day and putting on his green eyeshade and sitting there like a zombie for twelve or fourteen hours, doing not a goddam thing that anybody can figure out?

Maybe he was even going to print his memoirs on that little hand press of his.

The more I thought about it, the more irritated and indignant I got. For some reason, I couldn't get over it. I asked Betty, "What's he writing his memoirs about?"

She kind of stared at me out of her tired eyes, as if the question had never occurred to her. Then she put her elbow on the table beside the chair and bent her wrist with her hand in toward her neck, the way women do, and rested her chin on the back of her wrist.

"He told me why several times," she said, "but I'm not sure I can get it straight. I think it has something to do with the idea that the things that happen to him don't really exist—or don't fully exist—until he writes about them."

"My brother is crazy," I said. "Two Flee Police in Stolen Auto."

"I know it very well, but that isn't always important."

"What isn't?"

"Being crazy."

"But that isn't what I said. I said . . ."

But she interrupted me by snapping her fingers and saying, "Now I've got it. He has this idea that things don't fully exist unless they're expressed in symbols . . . you know, *symbolically*."

"Now what, for Christ's sake, does *that* mean?"

"Well," she said, "words are symbols, and I suppose . . ."

But she didn't finish telling me what she supposed. I think she believes Randall might be a genius or something, and she's steering a prudent course between belief and skepticism. One thing sure, though: she is crazy about the fat son of a bitch.

"I've seen that on some of the notes he leaves around the house," she said.

"You've seen what?" I asked her.

"That thing about symbols. I remember that."

"Swell," I said. "How long's he been writing these memoirs of his?"

"Oh, at least two months. At least, I think it's been that long."

"That boy," I said, "is a living, breathing, dyed-in-the-wool *fruitcake*. Nothing personal, even if he *is* your husband."

She just sat there and suffered for a while, with kind of a sad, bewildered smile on her wrinkly little face. Maybe wondering herself what Randall would have to put in his memoirs.

After she left, I still thought about this (Local Lunatic Pens Memoirs), alternating with wondering about Patti Nieder. Maybe Cripps would begin to write *his* memoirs. Maybe even Buckholz. And Yerby and Professor Homer Winslow and Sheila Richards and her husband, Phil, and T. F. Hanaway. And even my wife. (In Spanish, of course.)

Then I remembered something. That business about symbols and reality and how the latter doesn't fully exist without the former . . . all of that was Miss Temple's work. How could I have ever forgotten that shrewd old bitch, even for an instant? Wasn't I the cutup who would always stand up in the back row when she was facing the blackboard, talking about symbols, and move my fists up and down in long arcs, as if I were clanging cymbals together?

God, the charisma that beautiful old zombie had! What a woman! What a presence!

Local Teacher Remembered.

27

I was so damn surprised to hear about Randall writing his memoirs that I forgot all about the problem of letting him know that he was being trailed by Sheila's lunatic husband. The thought that Randall might be shot through his dirty sweatshirt in the gut by a jealous mulatto, Puerto Rican or whatever-he-was husband of a white woman was a curious thought.

I laid there for a couple hours, dozing and trying to get my vision squared away. Every now and then, some nurse would come by and give me a needle or a pill. And once, a young doctor came around and shined a light in my eyes and asked questions.

I was surprised that there were so few familiar faces around. I did see Dr. Tom Burchweinder, who used to be in Rotary. He came around a couple times and asked how I was doing; but he wasn't on my case, and he didn't waste much time. My charisma must have been practically nonexistent.

For the most part, I felt like hell. I laid there, aching and dizzy, and worried about that stupid son-of-a-bitch Randall and how I could tip him off without scaring the hell out of Betty. And I worried about Patti Nieder, and if I had believed in the mumbo jumbo, I would have said a prayer for her. I was feeling so low that, so help me, for a while I wished it would be me who died, rather than her, if one of us had to go. Or Gunther, who would be expendable in anyone's book.

That afternoon, there was a batch of mail came in. These things were addressed to the hospital. I got a letter in a plain envelope, just addressed to me at Room 354. So it was somebody who had called to find out where I was.

It was kind of childish handwriting, and it looked like a girl's. I opened the letter and read:

Hi there!

I am going to San Francisco with my husband. Things are just fine between us now, and this morning I was wondering what on earth we ever had to fight about. He understands everything, and that silly business about following you around is definitely over, especially since we will be living in San Francisco, which is a slightly more civilized place than this!

I do hope you recover quickly. I was so relieved to hear that you weren't hurt *too* badly.

Seriously, though: it has been a wonderful experience knowing you! You are a wonderful man, in your own particular way! I have never known a man who had a way with people the way you do. I think if I had seen you more recently, and if you had given me your "sales talk" the way you do, I would have been hypnotized. You could talk anybody into anything! Honestly!

Anyway, everything is working out for the best, I am sure. Before long, your wife will return from Spain. Maybe she is there now, and reading this letter! I hope so much she isn't, but I have to tell you these things in a letter, where everything is silent and I can tell the truth better than out loud. So I will do the imprudent thing, and mail it before I lose my nerve. Also, you-know-who will be returning shortly.

I am sure your wife is a wonderful woman. She would have

to be to deserve such a wonderful husband! I also hope and pray that the girl in the other car recovers.

Well, I have to stop now, or I could go on and on.

God Bless You,
You-Know-Who

Well, that was a pretty goddam silly letter, but it kind of affected me, and I laid there a while thinking about it.

It was shortly after reading Sheila's letter that I fell asleep and had a dream that was so vivid and so strange that I woke up in a sweat.

One thing about the dream was that it was all connected to everything around me. I mean, in the dream I heard that Patti Nieder had died, and I got up out of bed and walked down the ward to where her body was lying on a slab.

When I walked into the room, there were a bunch of doctors and nurses standing there, and they all stood aside while I walked up to the slab. "We want you to identify the body," a nurse said.

"But I've never seen the girl before," I told her.

"Yes, you have," she said. "You saw her the instant before the two cars hit, so you were the last person to see her alive. Her family and friends haven't seen her that recently, and she might have changed by that time."

Even in a dream, I considered this a silly thing to say, but I went up to the slab, nevertheless, and pulled back the white sheet.

And there was the nude corpse of Sheila Richards, lying on its back in a circle of light. Her body was covered with great purple bruises. Her hair was done up in a sparkly net, and her eyes were half open.

The rest of the room was dark, and suddenly there wasn't anybody else in it. "Why hasn't anybody closed her eyes?" I yelled. But nobody answered, so I closed them myself, and the face smiled.

Behind me, somebody said, "That *is* your wife, isn't it?"

Then I woke up, smelling chicken salad. The lunch tray was right beside my bed. A colored guy was standing there beside it, looking at me. For a second, I thought sure as hell it was Willie Byrd, but then I knew it couldn't be.

It must have been all the painkillers they had given me that made me confuse people with one another.

Then I began to think about Miss Temple. She had a kind of female charisma that was in a class all by itself. She was pretty, and fairly young when I had her in school; and she is still teaching, although she must be at least seventy now.

She was always talking about how everybody should keep a diary or a journal. I remember a couple of us one time tried to think of people who we figured had no business keeping one—garage men, shoe salesmen, soda jerks—but Miss Temple didn't back up an inch; she said everybody, and she meant *everybody*.

She would say that sometimes the best way to make sense out of things is to "write them down and let the wisdom of words, grammar and syntax help you out."

It's amazing how many things I could suddenly remember from Miss Temple's class. I could almost see her as she made that big, clean, efficient swallow—a faint smile on her face—and then said something like that, which would have sounded ridiculous coming from anybody else.

And naturally I realized that this must have been where Randall got his idea about writing his memoirs, because Randall had Miss Temple for an English teacher, too.

There was something else I remembered about Miss Temple then, and it came back to me with a shock.

It was on a Monday, after our high school had beaten its traditional rival, Greenville High, on the previous Friday night. It so happened that I had tackled one of their ends on the blind side, right after he'd taken in a little shovel pass over center. I really cold-cocked the poor son of a bitch, who was half a head taller than I was, but about twenty pounds lighter.

I gave him a concussion from that hard belt, and they had trouble bringing him around. They took him to the hospital and kept him there for observation a few days, and there was a lot of whispering among the students, and I was half taboo for a while. But he recovered.

Anyway, on this particular Monday, Miss Temple came up behind my desk (I always sat in the back row) and just stood there, while all of us were doing an in-class theme of some sort. After a while, I could smell her perfume and hear her breathing back there, and when I turned around, she was just standing there with her arms crossed and her head bent forward, staring at me meditatively.

Then she leaned over and whispered something in my ear that had to do with her sympathy over how bad I must feel at hurting this player. I couldn't exactly get her words straight, but I remember how puzzled I was afterwards, because I hadn't *really* felt guilty . . . and yet I was supposed to, obviously. My philosophy had always been, if you can't stand the lumps and the smell of sweat, don't bother putting on football equipment.

28

You just can't predict what's going to happen. There was a death in the hospital that night; but it wasn't Patti Nieder. It was Clendon Metzger, of all people, who died of a heart attack in his sleep.

They got me on my feet the next morning, and I walked

on crutches down to the visiting room, where I saw Mother Metzger. Her back was to me, and she was talking to an undertaker named Farley Gibbs.

I just stood there for a few minutes, but Farley didn't let on like he saw me, and of course Mother Metzger didn't turn around. She looked a little more stooped than when I had last seen her. Or at least, this is the way it seemed to me.

I hobbled on back to my room and sat there reading the newspaper and an old copy of *Field and Stream* for a while, and then it was lunchtime.

After lunch, I lit a Dutch Masters panetela and filled the room with smoke and read some more from the *Field and Stream*. Only, every now and then I would put the magazine down and just sit there gazing out the window.

At these moments, I would think of old Randall writing his memoirs, and I would think of Miss Temple, who had probably first put the idea into his head.

And then Sheila, and what she had said in that silly-ass letter about not being able to make sense out of things until she wrote them down. This was exactly what Randall was doing.

Farley Gibbs came in a few minutes later and said, "Hello there, Rex."

I told him hello, but that I didn't need his services just yet. Old Farley laughed politely, but it must have been the oldest joke in the world to him.

"I was just here to help Mrs. Metzger out," he said, and I told him I had seen him talking with her. Then I said, "Truck Driver Swerves to Avoid Child, Falls Off Sofa."

"She's taking it pretty well," Farley said, looking solemn. But I wasn't impressed by his solemn look, because I know how much money the bastard makes off of the misery of others, and I wasn't about to play sober with him.

"What are the last words you want to hear?" I asked him.

"What was that?" Farley said, turning his head a little to the side.

So I repeated the question, and he said, "What is this, Rex? Another joke?"

And I said, "Never mind, Farley. Just answer the goddam question."

So Farley looked dignified and said, "I don't know, Rex."

" 'Hello, deh. Ah is yoh new NEIGH-buh!' "

Old Farley tried to laugh a little, but it just came out as a little hum, and you could tell he was shocked that I would want to joke so soon after a paying customer had died.

A few minutes after that, Farley left. I was sleepy, so I took a nap. And when I woke up, the first person I saw was my wife, standing right there in the doorway, her eyes full of tears and a big silly smile on her face.

"Well I'll be goddamned," I said.

"Buenos días," she said. And then she broke out crying and ran over and threw her arms around my head. All the time she was sobbing and saying a lot of things that didn't make any sense. I was glad she had started talking English, however. And I did manage to get the impression that she was very glad to see me and happy that I was all right. Or at least alive.

For once in our married life, it was she who was too rough. She hugged me so hard that she hurt my ribs and shoulder—even with all the bandages around me. But I didn't say anything.

29

After they took me home in an ambulance, my wife clucked and cackled over me, and did everything but put me on the potty and sing me to sleep. She told me the story of a hotel fire in Madrid at least twenty times (although the nearest she was to danger was smelling smoke), and the episode about the German artist who told her fortune. Denise got a virus infection in a country village, and both of them polished their Spanish until they could express just about any silly idea that came into their two silly heads.

Patti Nieder has survived the accident, but it appears she will be paralyzed for the rest of her life. T. F. Hanaway is going to represent me, and he says I have a pretty good chance . . . that photographs and an investigation of the skid marks at the accident site show that it is possible that —even though I was intoxicated—I was driving within the requirements of the law.

I don't know. I might have been going five miles per hour too fast, and that might have made the difference. I do know that my car skidded, but now I'm not sure whether I skidded because we were going around the curve too fast, or because I was braking the car after seeing her car appear so suddenly.

Professor Homer Winslow has accepted a job teaching at a big university on the West Coast. I can't remember the name, but it's in California someplace. Maybe near Sheila and her husband in San Francisco. Who knows? He came to see me a couple of times, and he told me for the twentieth time he'd been on the verge of a nervous breakdown, and he kept saying what an influence around town, and/or the world, I could have been if things had been different. But of course things seem to work out for the best. I suppose this is because we adjust to whatever happens to us, and adjust to whatever we become, so that alternatives seem unnatural.

Gunther is all recovered and on the road somewhere with the Hatfield Four. My kids are all okay. My wife phoned them and told them I was not in danger, so they didn't have to come home. Personally, I doubt if they were intending to come home anyway, although I suppose they would have if I'd been dying. Maybe not.

I sat around the house for a couple of weeks, watching TV and reading the newspaper, *Outdoor Life, Sports Afield, Field and Stream,* and *Time,* until I thought I was about ready to go crazy. I'd call the lot three or four times a day and coach Bucky and Cripps on things. And they'd call home once or twice to ask questions. Sometimes one of them would drop by to have me check a deal.

Of course, people came to visit me. T. F. Hanaway, for one, and the Bonhams, the Klepingers, the Farrells, the Paulys. But one couple in particular: Vic Barnett, who is a lawyer, and his wife, Nancy.

They came in one afternoon about four o'clock, when I was just beginning to think about a Jack Daniel's. I was sitting on the patio, and I heard my wife start warbling a greeting, the way she does when somebody comes to the front door. And then Vic and Nancy were standing there in the big storm-door entrance at the back of the house, smiling and saying hello.

The surprise was when Nancy came up and put her hands on my side and gave me a big kiss. When I put my hands around her, one of them slid right down to her ass. It was just instinctive, I guess.

She stood back, smiling and saying how glad they both

were that I was getting along so well, and Vic shook his head and said, "Rex, you are a tough old rooster if I ever saw one," and my wife said, "Oh, he's tough, all right."

They had brought a couple bottles of cold duck for us, which my wife put in the refrigerator, and then Vic pitched in and fixed us all drinks, and we sat there and chatted in the late-afternoon shade of the patio.

After the talk had circled around a little bit here and there, Vic cleared his throat and said, "Rex, it's too bad about that girl, Patti Nieder."

"Yes, it sure is," I said.

"But I just wonder if you know about her," Vic said.

"Know what?"

"We don't know anything," my wife said quickly, her ears going to a point.

Vic kind of nodded and took another sip. "Well," he said, "she's one of the hippies at the college. She was living with some college boy out there in the country. I guess they lived in that big old house right on the other side of Liggett's place. You know where Liggett lives, don't you?"

I nodded and said I did.

"Well, they were renting that place from Clyde Milner, who'd given up on the damn thing as uninhabitable. I talked with the sheriff the other day, and he told me to let you know what they found out there so you wouldn't feel so bad and waste any time feeling guilty over the girl."

"What did they find?" my wife asked.

"Well, they were growing marijuana out in back of the house. The sheriff says that from all reports as to her habits, this Nieder girl might have been stoned when she was out driving and you hit her. No telling. Also, he said the inside of that house was filthy. Like a pigsty. He said if he'd known it was that bad, he would have worn a gas mask."

"What happened to her boy friend?" my wife asked.

"He took off right after the accident. Nobody knows

where he went. They had a little beagle pup out there that was dead by the time the sheriff went in. He figures it starved to death, or died of thirst."

"How awful," my wife said.

"Yes, a pretty sordid business," Vic said, rattling the ice cubes in his glass.

We sat there and chatted for at least another hour, and we were all feeling mellow by the time the Barnetts left.

I kept casting an eye on Nancy every now and then. I had always figured she was a damn attractive woman: not very breasty, but with an ass that was plump and round and very, very nice. And to think my hand had briefly rested upon it only a little while before.

And she had a pretty face, with wrinkly, sexy, good-natured eyes. She always did laugh a great deal, and shoot out little secret smiles at things when nobody else was looking.

Damn.

I wonder if my wife noticed?

Of course she did. In bed that night, she said, "Nancy certainly is attractive, isn't she? I think she's lovely."

I didn't say anything.

Men Communicate by Silence, Experts Say.

And Women by Questions.

30

Finally, I was well enough to trot around with a cane and drive a car. I had Bucky bring me up an almost new hardtop Corvette, which I immediately sold myself. It's a great little car—metallic green.

Then, the next day, I drove all over the county, checking out on things that are happening, and things that had happened since I'd been in the hospital. A man has to keep in touch.

T. F. asked me to write down as clearly as possible an account of the accident, not leaving anything out. So I went to Ted Spencer, who owns an office-supply store in town, and bought a new Smith-Corona model 220 electric typewriter. I had him deliver it to my office on the lot.

I took a course in typing in college, and it was one of my favorite courses. There's nothing like the feel of a clean sheet of paper when you turn it on the roller of a typewriter. As a matter of fact, I always did like to type, and up until a couple of years ago I would type my own stencils for our mimeographed specials we send out every week or so. Now, with the new typewriter, I could go back to doing this.

It was good getting back into the office, by God. I eased myself behind my desk and lit up a Dutch Masters panetela, and looked out over my stock. It didn't look too bad. Beyond the first row, I could see the metallic-green rear of my new Vette.

I picked up the phone and ordered some red roses for Patti Nieder, which I had been doing just about every day, and then I saw that the cup was empty of Marlboros. I called Cripps in and gave him a five, telling him to fill the goddam thing, and he took off in a ratty '68 Rambler, which they had taken in when I was still in the hospital.

I noticed that Bucky had circles under his eyes from the strain of command (or the strain of sharing it with Cripps), but otherwise he was the same old Bucky. Willie Byrd came over and shot the bull with us for a while, and seeing him made me think of Sheila's husband. I was thinking, Willie Byrd was not over half colored, and if he was to knock up a white woman, their kid would be about the color of Sheila's husband. Son of a bitch.

I sat there at the desk all afternoon, typing up my version of the accident. Then I put it in an envelope and mailed it to T. F. Hanaway, who undoubtedly had a new secretary by now.

The next day, the typewriter was still there and I began to think about Randall writing his memoirs, and then I began to think about the things that had happened to me over the past few months. I was trying to think of what they all added up to, and then I realized that I couldn't really know until I got them into some kind of order.

So I started writing this account, which of course I will not let my wife see. I don't want to hurt her feelings, because, as a matter of fact, I'm crazy about her.

Now it is October, and the weather is beautiful—cool and sunny both. The cars look so bright and shiny, you can almost close your eyes and see them.

I've gone over the things I have written, and some of them don't seem quite right. But I'm not changing anything, because everything I wrote down was exactly the way it seemed to me at the time, and why should I come back now and think that I can make it more accurate?

Miss Temple was right: during the course of my writing, I've had to do a lot of thinking about Winslow and Sheila and Bucky and Cripps and Gunther and Yerby and Patti Nieder. And my wife.

I think that Professor Homer Winslow has a good point, underneath all the bullshit. I mean, we're all in the charisma business. What is my wife trying to do except exercise her magic life style on me and make me turn into some glamorous goddam Spaniard? (Only she's let up on this lately; but never mind, she'll think of something else.) And Sheila, playing the oldest female game of them all, trying to exercise her charisma on me through the language of glances and hairdo and touch titty and all that sort of thing. And now maybe Nancy Barnett. Who knows?

And then there are Bucky and Cripps, pretending to be loyal and true . . . giving me the old business about how great I am, which I am foolish enough to believe until that day when I am curled up in the VW Microbus, thinking of dying from a hangover, and hear what they really think of me. And then my boy, Phil, the poor addleheaded son of a bitch, who's convinced he's been to the goddam mountaintop and anybody who has the bad luck to be older should listen to his wisdom.

And so it goes, on and on. Maybe even Randall, with his printing press and his memoirs. Why not? And even that Christmas turkey, Professor Homer Jerry Winslow, trying to convert me into Adlai Stevenson or Eugene McCarthy or some similar damn body.

Yes, we're all caught up in the charisma game, flashing out these signals from inside our heads, trying to knock everybody dead and trying not to get infected by the poisonous needle of *their* charisma.

Clowns and fools, that's what we all are. But the game is beautiful, and it is sure as hell fun, if you see it right and understand that it *is* a goddam game, and understand that anybody who doesn't think we're all crazy is crazy.

31

One day Bucky came up to me while I was typing this account, and he said, "Rex, just whatcha doing, typing all the time?"

"I'm writing my memoirs," I told him.

"You're what?" he asked.

"Writing my memoirs."

"What's 'at?" he said.

"An account of my life," I said.

He looked at my eyebrows a second, and then nodded slowly and switched the toothpick from one side of his mouth to the other.

When he left the office, I printed a sign with my felt-tipped marker that said, "Where there's life there's hope, and sometimes even where there isn't." But the marker was almost dry.

Then I had a by-God sudden inspiration and got a fresh Scripto pen out of the desk and took the cap off. I tested the felt point, and it was full of rich black ink. So I took out a blank piece of cardboard and printed "Rex McCoy, King of Kars!" I looked at it a second, and then added two more exclamation marks.

I turned the sign all around and looked at it this way and that. Not bad. I'd get gold-colored crowns made for Cripps and Bucky and myself, and, by God, we could even get long purple robes with gold tassles. I'd get a wand for each one of us.

When Bucky asked me about it, which he would surely do, I'd say, "Rex means 'king' in latin, my boy, and you'd goddam better believe it, because we're going to make *them* believe it!"

God, I'd knock this town on its ass!

The other day I bought a fine cane. I can walk real well with it now, and I feel like a million dollars.

I go down the street wearing my string tie and swinging my cane, and people look up when they see me and smile. They don't seem to hold the Patti Nieder thing against me, I'm happy to say. Even if they know about it.

This is a great little town, and I love it.

I can imagine them saying, There's old Rex, the son of a bitch. He's a real character, that jasper is, but he could talk the President of the United States into buying Russian imperial bonds.

That's the kind of man I happen to be, and I don't mind admitting it.

Local Dealer Accepts Self.

Critics Claim Issue Never in Doubt.